Lucy Morris lives in Essex, UK, with her husband, two young children and two cats. She has a massive sweet tooth and loves gin, bubbly and Irn-Bru. She's a member of the UK Romantic Novelists' Association. She was delighted to accept a two-book deal with Harlequin after submitting her story to the Warriors Wanted! submission blitz for Viking, medieval and Highlander romances. Writing for Harlequin Historical is a dream come true for her and she hopes you enjoy her books!

Sarah Rodi has always been a hopeless romantic. She grew up watching old romantic movies recommended by her grandad or devouring love stories from the local library. Sarah lives in the village of Cookham in Berkshire, where she enjoys walking along the River Thames with her husband, her two daughters and their dog. She has been a magazine journalist for over twenty years, but it has been her lifelong dream to write romance for Harlequin. Sarah believes everyone deserves to find their happy-ever-after. You can contact her via @sarahrodiedits or sarahrodiedits@gmail.com. Or visit her website at sarahrodi.com.

CONVENIENT VOWS WITH A VIKING

———

Lucy Morris
Sarah Rodi

HARLEQUIN
HISTORICAL

HARLEQUIN®

HISTORICAL™

Recycling programs
for this product may
not exist in your area.

ISBN-13: 978-1-335-59599-7

Convenient Vows with a Viking

Copyright © 2024 by Harlequin Enterprises ULC

Her Bought Viking Husband
Copyright © 2024 by Lucy Morris

Chosen as the Warrior's Wife
Copyright © 2024 by Sarah Rodi

For questions and comments about the quality of this book,
please contact us at CustomerService@Harlequin.com.

Harlequin Enterprises ULC
22 Adelaide St. West, 41st Floor
Toronto, Ontario M5H 4E3, Canada
www.Harlequin.com

Printed in U.S.A.

CONTENTS

HER BOUGHT
VIKING HUSBAND

Lucy Morris

For my friend Sue (Virginia Heath), thank you for being so supportive and sharing your wisdom so freely.

Dear Reader,

Iceland was a land of hope and political freedom for many in the Viking Age. But it is important to note the thralls who were forcibly taken there from Britain and Ireland. In fact, evidence suggests a 50/50 split between Nordic and Gaelic settlers (with most Gaelic DNA being female). I wanted to share a story about one such Irish woman. *Icelanders in the Viking Age* by William R. Short was an informative read when researching this time and place.

Chapter One

Southern district, Iceland—AD 910

'I need a husband,' Orla admitted with a heavy sigh.

Gunnar appeared not to have heard her, or more likely he did not *want* to hear her. He concentrated on driving their horse and cart, his eyes fixed on the muddy path and flatlands ahead.

'Someone I can trust,' she added pointedly, turning a little in her seat to see him better.

Gunnar wasn't exactly her ideal choice of husband. He was missing his front teeth, and had seen over fifty winters, which was at least twenty more than herself. But he was a good-hearted and honourable man, a rare commodity in this unforgiving land.

'No,' Gunnar replied firmly, without even bothering to meet her eye.

She sucked in a deep breath, ready to set out all the reasons why it was the perfect solution to all their problems... Well, *her* problems. 'But—'

Immediately he interrupted her. '*But* I agree, you need to marry. Not me, of course, but someone.'

Orla stared up at the gulls wheeling in the overcast sky—they were freer than her. Indulging her frustration, she let out a loud piercing scream.

'Curse you, Skalla!' she yelled, spitting her words at the mountain in the distance. The lands beneath it were owned by her uncle—she despised every pebble and blade of grass that lived there. 'May your guts rot and your eyes fall out!'

Gunnar gave a light snort of amusement. 'If he ever hears you cursing him, he will *definitely* have good reason to take your lands.'

'Good reason? That old goat has no right to anything and he knows it! Ever since Father died, he has been itching to take my farm. How many labourers has he already taken from me? I am surprised he did not try to steal you! He thinks to cut me down, piece by piece, as if my land were a joint of ham! Does he think he can strip me bare without anyone noticing?'

'They notice,' Gunnar said unhappily, 'but what can they do? He is a *godi*… Untouchable.'

Orla couldn't argue with Gunnar's reasoning. Skalla was one of the elders. An important and influential voice on the island. Many men were sworn to him by oath and as the *godi*—the voice of the district—his word was final.

If Orla went against him, she risked bringing an army down upon her head. Already he had taken her vote in the assembly by claiming he held it by proxy.

Women were forbidden from meetings, but surely it was up to her who cast her vote?

Apparently not.

Nothing seemed to be her choice any more.

However, *that* was only a minor insult compared to what Skalla had done recently. Two weeks ago, he had moved his livestock to graze on her land. He had done it brazenly and without apology, as if he were entitled to it, allowing his cattle to grow fat on her hay fields, hay that she had planned to feed to her own animals during the long winter months.

After much ranting, Skalla had eventually admitted his *mistake* and promised her some of his own hay supplies in recompense. But she doubted they would ever arrive. The harvesting had begun and, so far, she had received nothing.

What would she do without enough hay to last the winter?

She would be forced to slaughter animals needlessly, or otherwise watch them starve. It was a choice she shouldn't have to make and the injustice of it all made her blood boil.

Folding her hands in her lap, she muttered, 'Surely he has enough! Why must he have my lands, too? He *knows* Oddr meant for me to have the farm. He even promised Father he would look after me. *Black-hearted liar!*'

Gunnar shook his head. 'In his head, he *is* keeping his word.'

Frowning at Gunnar's odd statement, she snapped, 'Nonsense. He is greedy and always has been.'

'Some men do not believe women capable of running such a large farm alone. As there is no man in your household, he is within his rights to claim your lands as his own. But he has not done so *yet*, which bodes well...'

Gunnar's words of reason only infuriated her further. 'Only because Father told *everyone* that he planned for me to inherit. To go against my father's last wishes would mean Skalla losing favour with the people and the gods. Instead, he thinks to steal it away slowly, all while feigning concern... He is truly the *vilest* of men!'

'*Still...*' Gunnar said so much with that single word.

Orla sat back defeated, anger flowing away like a receding tide, leaving only misery in its wake. 'I am not my father's daughter by blood.'

Gunnar's face filled with sympathy. 'To all of us you are Oddr's child... But some will say that Skalla has more right to claim the land as he is his brother.'

'Skalla agreed to my inheritance,' she grumbled, already feeling as if she had lost the war. Shrugging, she added, 'Besides, he is not my only problem. The lost sheep, the damage to the barn... There is no proof they were *all* done by Skalla, so there could be others who wish me harm.'

'True...and I fear that this will only be the beginning. Perhaps you should marry Skalla's son? No one would object, as you are not blood relatives, and you would be safer with his name as your shield...' Even as Gunnar made the suggestion, he grimaced as if the words turned his stomach.

'I would rather bathe in the boiling swamp than

marry Njal!' Orla snorted, then gave Gunnar a pleading look. 'Will you not at least *consider* marrying me?'

Gunnar rolled his eyes. 'What would marrying me
give you? Other than the title of widow far too soon.'

When she opened her mouth to argue, he wagged
his finger at her. 'And do not fan my pride with false
words. I am not young, and though I be a freeman, I
have no powerful connections or family to speak of.
If you married me, someone would come and cut off
both our heads without a moment's hesitation and claim
your lands for themselves. Even Skalla would be unable to intervene once you married out of his family.
You must either pick Njal, or a man similar. Anyone
less and you will be dead before the end of the year.'

Gunnar was always a pessimistic man, but in this
case he was not wrong.

Orla thought long and hard before answering. 'You
are right. Although I fear Njal would be little improvement over death.'

'But he would be an improvement.'

Orla remained silent; she wasn't so certain. She had
seen how Njal treated his thralls. He abused and discarded them easily, viewing them as nothing more than
tools or toys to be used until they were broken. He did
not see them as people. Orla did, because she had once
been a slave herself, and she did not trust that her life
with Njal would ever be happy…or long.

When Gunnar and Orla arrived at the trading centre
under Kaldbakr mountain, they stopped by the merchants' square first to sell their woollen cloth. As this

was one of the last weeks of the summer, the merchants would soon leave for the eastern markets of Jorvik and Birka.

Deliberately she had left selling her cloth until late in the season when the merchants' purses would be fat and they would be eager to buy something to take back with them.

As such, her cloth was sold quickly, for a heavy purse of silver. Eager to leave, the merchant was already instructing his crew to load it on to his ship. Orla always received a good price for her wool. Her farm was prosperous, with many cows and sheep, as well as plenty of fields for grain and hay.

But her main income came from her cloth production. With so many women working the looms, her fleeces—as well as those of some of her neighbours who traded with her—were quickly turned into bolts of fabric. Over the years she had gained a reputation for producing the finest cloth.

No one ever suspected the real reason why she focused on weaving over grain or meat production—only the people who worked for her knew the truth.

While she waited for the cart to be unloaded, she let her eyes roam over the market and jetty. A slave ship was currently being unloaded, which was unusual as it was late in the season for arrivals, and her eyes couldn't help but be drawn to the miserable souls being pulled from it.

'That was me once…'

Orla hadn't realised she had spoken aloud until Gunnar patted her shoulder kindly with a gum-filled smile. 'You were lucky.'

She nodded, her eyes returning to the long rope of people.

Lucky.

She had been little more than a babe when she arrived on this shore. Her memories were vague, but she remembered clinging on to a cold stranger's hand, stumbling down the ramp and then climbing up the large steps to the auction block. She had been taken from Ireland, in one of the many raids of her motherland, and brought to these remote shores like cattle. Her parents had died in the raid. She could not remember their faces, or even whose hand she had held.

Thankfully, she did not remember much from the raid. Smoke, chaos and a terrible storm… She still hated the sound of thunder, even now. But no memory was clear…which was probably a blessing.

However, she did remember Oddr buying her. How the stranger's hand had let go of her so easily and then been replaced by his warm one.

She *had* been lucky that day.

It was why she had taken to buying slaves with any spare silver she had. She freed them immediately and they usually worked her land or looms until the debt of buying them was repaid. Very rarely did they choose to leave after, but most had nothing to return to and wished only to build a new life in peace.

'Keep the silver,' Gunnar warned quietly. 'You should use it as a dowry…or save it for more hay this winter. You can't help them…not today.'

Gunnar was right. She could not afford another mouth to feed this winter, not with her hay supplies at risk, and, if she needed a husband, she would need a fat dowry to entice a man into standing up against Skalla and Njal.

People were depending on her to make the right decision.

She should look away from the slaves being unloaded. There was little she could do to help. But it was as if she enjoyed torturing herself, because she watched them anyway, knowing that someone who cared should at least bear witness to their suffering.

Three young men, with slim builds and hollow stomachs, slowly walked down the ship's ramp and on to the jetty. They did not look as if they had been treated well. Bruises bloomed over their dirty bodies and they were painfully thin. She imagined this wasn't their first time on the selling block. Sometimes slaves were passed from market to market until they found a master. Iceland was one of the lands at the edge of the world, so she dreaded to think how long they had been passed around.

Two women came next. Wretched, frightened-looking creatures, who walked with stooped shoulders, afraid to show off their bodies or pride. Untidy brown hair falling in front of their faces like dead weeds. Both the young men and women all looked Saxon by their clothing, which was badly torn and stained, although the women's seemed a little better, suggesting they were newly captured compared to the men.

Her heart hurt to look at them and she was about

to force her gaze away when the last slave emerged. This man was huge and in far better condition than the others. He was blond, tall and built for battle. The runes tattooed over his arms and bare chest confirmed it.

'What is a Norse warrior doing as a slave?'

Gunnar shrugged. 'Norse settlements are sometimes raided by warring jarls…'

'He doesn't seem the type to be captured in a raid.'

'True…he does look like a warrior. Maybe he offended the King?'

Orla watched in fascination as the warrior shuffled awkwardly down the ramp. One of the slavers prodded him with a spear as if he were a bear to be baited. His hands and feet were naked and bound with chains, not rope like the rest of the thralls. There were bruises and cuts all over his body as if he had been in a terrible fight. The light brown trousers he wore were once fine, with a rich embroidered belt, but now they were covered in blood and ripped in several places. Most of the blood was not his own, she realised, and she shivered.

How many died to capture such a man?

His hair was cropped at the sides, but long on top, and currently fell down in front of his eyes. Whatever he might have used to tie it back was long gone. His shaggy beard hid most of his face from view, but he looked around him with the arrogance of a man who was not used to such treatment.

The woman in front of him stumbled and he instinctively reached for her. Even though his hands were shackled and mostly useless to him, he still managed to grab her dress and pull her upright.

The woman turned a little and gave a small nod of thanks before hurrying forward, fearful that she would be pulled over again by the rope that led them. The blond man did not seem to care if he failed to keep up—despite the threat of the spear at his back. His eyes roamed around the trading square as if calculating his next move, and, when his blue eyes met hers, she almost flinched at the murderous intent reflected in them.

He was kind to his fellow slaves, but he would offer no mercy to any other. It was an oddly comforting thought.

Orla's hand drifted to the heavy weight of her purse at her belt.

Perhaps there was a better use for her coin...

Chapter Two

Hakon looked around him at the desolate country he had found himself in. There was a cold whip in the air despite it being late summer. The land was full of extremes: flat beaches and farmland, with huge black peaks bursting up from the earth in the distance.

Beautiful but harsh.

He had heard tales that Iceland was a land that spat fire and ice in equal measure. In his mind, it was not a hospitable place; people came here only as a last resort when they had fallen out of favour with the King.

Hakon had never imagined he would step foot on its miserable shores.

Curse Jarl Ingvar!

If he killed the man a thousand times, it would *still* not be enough to ease his thirst for vengeance!

As soon as he was free, Hakon would go back and gut the bastard. He had spent the last few weeks of his captivity imagining all the ways he would torture and destroy the man who had sold him into slavery.

It would have been better, at least for Ingvar, if he had just killed him.

As it was, he had Ingvar's sister, Sigrid, to thank for this miserable existence. She had been the one to convince her brother that killing him without trial would only anger King Harald.

'It would not be wise to kill him, Brother. Sell him into slavery instead—he will be as good as dead, but without his blood staining your hands. You can say that Hakon accepted it as punishment for his brothers' crimes. Besides...many ships are lost during the crossing to Iceland. Not only that, I have also heard the life of an Icelandic thrall is notoriously hard and short. You would be considered blameless if he died and then his brothers will still have to face trial with King Harald. Their reputation and power will be destroyed regardless. Hakon will never return to dispute your claims and, even if he did, so much time would have passed that his injustice would be easily forgotten... At least by the King.'

Hakon had wanted to wring her neck when she had said that, but later he had wondered if there was more to it.

Sigrid had given him bread and water before he left and had even begged for his mercy in the future. It seemed she had more sense than her ambitious brother. She probably realised Ingvar would never get away with his deceit and hoped to protect herself by helping Hakon.

After all, King Harald would be enraged to learn of the killing of one of his best men without trial. The blood feud between Ingvar's and Hakon's families had been burning for several generations. But as Hakon became more popular with the King, Ingvar had grown afraid that his position as jarl was at risk.

The King had ordered a marriage alliance between Ingvar's sister and Hakon. But when Hakon and his brothers had gone to negotiate the terms, thinking they were protected by the laws of hospitality, they were quickly betrayed, waking up to find blades at their throats.

Ingvar claimed his sister had been raped by his brothers and demanded immediate retribution. All lies, of course, which were obvious to everyone there. Before Ingvar could order their immediate execution, Hakon had wrestled a weapon from one of the guards, freeing himself and his brothers.

They had fought wildly to break out of Ingvar's hall and return to their ship. His brothers had made it out at least. Hakon only prayed Odin had protected his brothers' retreat.

Grimr's wounds had been deep and Egill had barely been able to walk after his head wound. Hakon wasn't even sure if they had managed to get back to the ships, or if they had died trying. Sigrid had told him they'd escaped…but could he trust her?

At least Hakon had done everything in his power to give them time to escape, fighting as savagely as a berserker to stop anyone from following them.

He had sent several of Ingvar's men into the afterlife, despite initially being unarmed, and he took some comfort in that. If Sigrid had not hit him from behind, knocking him out, he might have killed even more.

If nothing else, Hakon had ruined Ingvar's plans.

He had probably hoped to kill them all before the trial of his sister's supposed rape. King Harald would only have heard of the crime and their attempted escape. There would be no reason to blame Ingvar for killing men who fled from judgement. But now with Hakon's brothers free, there would be another story to tell, one that conflicted with Ingvar's tale.

If his brothers had survived…

Curse Jarl Ingvar and his deceitful sister!

His thoughts circled back, like a serpent eating its own tail. For weeks he had been locked within the swirling darkness of his own rage.

But then a splash of colour caught his attention as he made his way towards the auction block. A woman with a crescent of red hair, just visible beneath a linen cap. A halo of fire in a desolate land, reminding him of some of the Christian paintings he had seen, with golden moons surrounding saints' faces. It fascinated him to see something similar in the flesh—he had always thought Christian art ridiculous until now.

Despite the modesty of her cap, the redhead's hair refused to be subdued. The wind had pushed the cloth further back, allowing some of her flaming locks to escape and frame her pale, freckled face. She wasn't pretty, but she wasn't ugly either. There was a strength to the line of her jaw that spoke of confidence and grit. She wasn't young, probably the same age as himself, which made sense considering she wore her hair like a married woman and stood next to a much older man.

He wished he were closer so that he could see the colour of her eyes more clearly. She did not seem to fear anyone around her, even though she was small in stature. Her cloak was wrapped around her tightly and embroidered prettily, but without the usual silk he was used to seeing on a noble woman, and she did look noble…although…not Norse nobility.

A Celt, probably—he had heard many women had been taken from their homelands to work in Iceland. But she did not look like a thrall either and he should know, having joined the ranks of such unfortunate souls.

He was so distracted by his thoughts that it took him a moment to realise the woman was staring back at him. Normally, he was used to the attention of women, but he didn't like it now, not in his current wretched state. Shame clawed up his face and neck, but he refused to look away.

Let her look, he would not live this way for long!

He would win his freedom or die trying.

He lined up with the rest of the thralls as they waited for their turn on the auction block. The merchant had said he was keen to sell all of them and return home with silver rather than more mouths to feed.

Hakon did not care who bought him, as he would not be a thrall for long. He would escape, leave this wretched island somehow and then he would seek his revenge. Even if it took months or years, he would pay Ingvar back for this humiliation.

Ingvar would one day wish he *had* killed him.

Hakon was distracted from his wrathful thoughts by the tug of the rope that was connected to his shackles. The merchant was talking with several buyers who were inspecting them with interest.

Two large men were pawing at Mildritha and Wynflaed. They flinched at the intrusive touches of the
men, as they tugged at their hair and examined their
teeth. He pitied the two sisters.

They had been unlucky, captured by the merchant as
they walked along the coast of northern England. The
merchant hadn't even planned to carry more people, but
he had seen them before they had had a chance to escape and he had gathered them up like driftwood. They
had fought hard, but it had been useless in the end.

The other thralls were men who had been sold repeatedly and had probably not been much more than
labourers prior to their captivity. They accepted their
fate with dull eyes and no argument.

Hakon had a new appreciation for the hardships
of thralls that he had never expected to learn first-
hand. He had grown used to Mildritha and Wynflaed.
They had been good to him and had even tended his
wounds whenever they could. He hoped they would
not be treated unkindly by their new master. Unfortunately, the leering looks of the men currently viewing
them told a darker tale.

He glared at the men until they noticed him and with
grumbled muttering they moved on. It was then that
he noticed someone was stood in front of him—it was
the red-haired woman he had noticed before.

He could see now that her eyes were green. A soft
mossy colour that looked eerily piercing in her pale face.

'Are you Norse?' she asked and there was no Celtic
lilt in her accent, which only confused him further.

Hakon thought it a stupid question, but he nodded

anyway, proudly straightening his spine to show how clearly Norse he was. 'I was once Jarl Hakon Eriksson, until Ingvar the Bald captured me and sold me into slavery. I was betrayed by a man who broke the laws of hospitality and honour. I will not rest until I have my vengeance.' His speech was stiff and cold—he had repeated it in his head many times during the journey here.

Her eyes widened, but she spoke carefully as if considering her words before speaking. 'You were once a warrior, then?'

That irritated him. 'I am *still* a warrior,' he growled.

What had he expected? That he would reveal his name and status and be immediately freed?

The merchant laughed. 'He is proud. You will need to use a firm hand to get the best out of him. I have whipped and beaten him, but he is still as arrogant as the day he was given to me in chains. You might suit one of the others better, Lady Orla. They are far more biddable and I know how you like to take on women for your looms.'

The merchant gestured to Mildritha and Wynflaed. But Lady Orla did not look away from Hakon, her eyes searching his face for something, although he had no idea what.

A lady, but with a name like Orla she was definitely a Celt, despite her lack of accent. A concubine raised up to the title of wife, perhaps? That made sense, especially in such a remote land as this, and the man beside her was much older. The kind of man that might be persuaded to marry a slave.

The merchant was called away by another customer

and he was left to stare into moss-coloured eyes and wonder what she was thinking. The older man, he presumed her husband, came to stand beside her.

Hakon noticed his front teeth were missing when he spoke. 'Mistress, I know what you are considering and I would advise against it.'

That piqued Hakon's interest and not only because it proved they were not married. 'What are you considering? Do you need a man killed? I will do it, if you swear to free me after.'

Her eyes saddened a little. 'Killing one man might not be enough.'

It was probably not wise for him to tell her of his plans for escape. But a part of him hoped she would not buy him. He could not be her protector; he would only betray her and escape at the first opportunity. 'I have no wish to remain a slave. You would do better to buy the women, like the merchant suggested. I will never accept the life of a thrall.'

Her head tilted as if measuring his words. 'I know what it is to be in your position. I was lucky enough to be bought by a good man who freed me and wanted nothing in return. But I am only a woman and cannot afford such generosity. If I buy you and free you, I will expect something in return.'

'Mistress…' pleaded the man beside her.

'What do you want?' Hakon asked without hesitation. He would slaughter a hundred men to regain his freedom.

She lifted that sharp jaw of hers and stared him straight in the eyes. 'I need a husband.'

Chapter Three

Hakon said nothing. He stared at her with wide blue eyes that were prettier than the hot lagoon not far from here.

Of course, nothing else about him was pretty.

Handsome, yes. Terrifyingly strong and fierce? Also, yes. But that was what she needed, wasn't it?

'I will begin the auction soon,' called the merchant from his block and her heart quickened with panic. Gunnar looked as if he wanted to weep and was already cursing under his breath at her recklessness. But Orla had never been more certain. It defied reason, but she trusted the man in front of her. She believed he was essentially good and would solve her problems with Skalla.

'Will you do it?' she asked.

'Marry you?' he replied, his brow creased with confusion.

'Yes!' she snapped, a little frustrated by his slowness. 'You are not dim-witted, are you?' she asked, a little worried. After all, he *had* managed to let himself get captured.

'No… Are *you*?' His eyes narrowed and he leaned forward, the chains rattling as he moved, reminding her of his current position and the oddness of her request. 'I will not stay here!'

She nodded and spoke quickly, afraid that she would run out of time. 'I understand. But you will need a ship, will you not? Or at least enough silver to buy you passage home. I am not wealthy. I will have to use most of my silver just to buy you. But I can eventually give you enough to buy passage home…'

The group of slaves shuffled forward as the auctioning of the male thralls began and Orla had to walk with him a few steps.

'You will not be able to leave until spring at the earliest anyway. That will be enough time to prove yourself as my husband and protector. Then you can go. You need only come back occasionally over the years to remind them of your claim. And, if you *really* are a jarl, then you can send men to be my guards in your stead—a handful would do.'

They were so close to the block now that the women in front of Hakon were beginning to climb it and she began to whisper so that the merchant would not hear her. 'I will be your wife, but you do not need to remain here. You could leave and pretend it never happened. What say you? Are you willing to give up a few months of freedom in return for guaranteed vengeance?'

'Fine.' Hakon looked down at her with a grim expression that almost made her wonder if he would refuse her. But then he dragged up his bound hands and thumped them awkwardly against his heart. 'I swear, I will marry you and give you protection, even after I am gone from here… But you must buy the women, too.'

She glanced nervously at the two women who were standing on the steps ahead of him. 'I might not have enough for all three of you…'

His eyes were as cold as the ocean when he met her gaze. 'You can buy me, make me your husband, whatever you wish. But if you want me to send you men and guarantee your protection for the rest of your life…you will pay for it by saving theirs.' He gestured with his chin to the frightened women ahead of him and she nodded in agreement before stepping away.

When she placed her first bid on one of the women, she heard rumbles of disagreement from some of the men gathered in front of the auction. As always, she ignored them and won the first woman easily.

But when she bid on the second, Snorri turned to her and snapped angrily, 'Must you buy every woman that comes to our shores? Surely, you should be spending it on protecting your land instead of wasting it on yet more weavers!'

Orla had never liked Snorri. He obviously disapproved of her lack of a husband, as he had advised her father several times to get her *wedded and bedded*. He was her neighbour and she had been wondering recently if he was the culprit who had been stealing her sheep.

Disgusted, she shrugged. 'Take your pick from the next ships to come in. I won't be back here for months anyway.'

'What ships? It is nearing the end of the season.'

Snorri spat on the ground at her feet, but she ignored him and won the final bid on the two women.

'Now look at this thrall—a rare find!' shouted the merchant, tugging Hakon forward. 'Raise your arms!' he ordered, jabbing him with the handle of his whip.

Hakon raised his arms over his head, the movement highlighting the rippling muscles of his biceps and stomach. The pectorals on his chest contracting like sheets of sculpted rock, he looked as strong as an ox. 'This man would make a fine worker or fighter. Need a woodland cleared—he will do it in half the time. A field ploughed? He can do it alone. Or, why not entertain your guests at your next feast by making him your challenger?'

The merchant appeared oblivious to the murderous glare Hakon gave him. The group of buyers pressed forward a little as if to take a better look. Orla smiled to herself—even though the crowd seemed interested, she doubted anyone would actually pay for him. Not because Hakon wasn't capable of such feats—it was obvious he was—but who would wish to deal with a man so obviously full of rage?

It wasn't that long ago that a group of thralls had risen up against their master and killed him in his sleep. No, no one would take the risk with a slave capable of killing them with their bare hands.

Orla raised her hand and made a small offer—maybe she could still buy the extra hay after all.

To her surprise Snorri stepped forward. 'You say he can fight? Maybe I will pit my house bear against him at the autumn blot? Bjarni Bear could do with a challenge…'

Murmurs of interest sang around the square. Snorri had bought a white bear cub from a Greenlander a few winters ago and he dragged out the poor beast each year to battle dogs or men depending on how much they had had to drink. Orla had complained more than once about the wild beast, insisting such dangerous pets should be banned on the island. She and Snorri had argued fiercely over it at the last feast.

At least the bear had never been badly harmed. Snorri wouldn't allow it.

Odin's teeth, how he loved Bjarni Bear! Treated it like a baby, with its own sleeping quarters and only the best meat and fresh hay for its bedding. She was surprised he would risk its life with someone like Hakon.

When she saw the smirk on Snorri's face, however, she realised he was deliberately driving up the price just to annoy her.

Orla swallowed the ball of nerves and tried to pretend she didn't feel the diminishing weight of her purse.

Had she made a mistake? Too late, she had cast her dice, only the Norns knew her fate now.

She raised her hand and several men, including Snorri, turned and looked at her as if she had lost her mind. 'I will pay double.' He was notorious for being tight-fisted when it came to his silver and she hoped her high bid would put him off from making another. She couldn't afford anything more and he would not risk being landed with an expensive slave he did not want.

Snorri walked forward and inspected Hakon thought-

fully, no doubt just to irritate her further. 'Do you think
he could win against a bear?'

'Of course!' The merchant laughed.

'But will he do as he is told? I want no trouble.'

The merchant's smile faltered a little, but then he
poked Hakon in the ribs with the handle of his whip.
'With the right training. You could make him do any—'
The merchant's words were cut off as Hakon slammed
his arms down against the whip and it dropped to the
floor. Snorri jumped back several feet with a yelp.

However, Hakon was not finished. He still had the
merchant's arm pinned to his stomach and he grabbed
the man's tunic sleeve to hold the merchant in place as
he slammed his head with a hideous crack against the
merchant's nose.

Blood sprayed across the floor and the merchant
let out a scream of pain as he crumpled to the wooden
floor of the auction block, cupping his face.

The merchant's guards flew up the steps with spears
in hand and Orla rushed forward, her hands raised in
a desperate plea. 'I will still buy him! But only if he is
unharmed! Double Snorri's offer, remember!'

The merchant, realising he could be left without a
sale, halted his guards with a raised hand and stumbled
to his feet. Hakon did not move, as if his sudden violence had never happened. It was chilling to see; he had
not even broken into a sweat.

The merchant tried to laugh, but he choked a little on
the blood pouring from his nose. 'Ha-uh-ha… Snorri,
is it? See…he is a powerful man. He will make a good

challenger for your bear. Surely you will not miss out on this opportunity to a woman?'

Snorri took another step back. 'No, I will pass. I would rather *she* die at his hands than either myself or my Bjarni Bear. I will gladly let her have him!'

The merchant patted at his nose with a cloth and nodded. 'As you wish. I hope you have your silver ready, Mistress. I want this man gone from my sight as soon as possible.'

Orla hurried forward and paid the man, and the three slaves were quickly handed to her, the rope pressed into her hands like a lead.

'What are your names?' she asked the two women, who kept their eyes low.

'I am Mildritha and this is Wynflaed…we are sisters,' said the braver of the two.

'Can you weave wool?'

Both sisters nodded, although Wynflaed glanced at her sister with a worried expression.

'I have high standards. So, you will be taught the proper technique whether you have experience or not.' Wynflaed seemed to relax a little at Orla's words. 'Now, I say this to every thrall who comes to my hall. I have a large farm. Everyone must work hard to ensure we are prosperous and well fed through winter. Which is why I do not keep thralls…they have no incentive to work hard.'

Both women looked up at her with wide eyes and Orla continued without pausing. 'Which is why you are no longer thralls, but my bondswomen. I expect one hundred ells of fine cloth in payment for buying you, or at least a year of work. Once your debt is paid, you may stay as one of my paid women, marry or leave whenever you wish. Any bad behaviour will increase your debt and good behaviour will reduce it. Is that clear?'

Both women nodded quickly. 'Yes, Mistress.'

Orla took a step forward, her voice hushed. 'You may call me Orla at home…but always Mistress, or Mistress Orla, when we are in public. There are many who do not approve of how I run my farm and, believe me, you would not wish to end up with them. Do you understand?'

Both women lowered their heads obediently. 'Yes, Mistress.'

'Good. Gunnar, untie these women and take them to our cart. We will leave shortly.'

'What do you expect me to do with him?' Gunnar said grimly, gesturing at Hakon, who had been moved to the side of the auction block by one of the merchant's guards. Her soon-to-be husband was staring at the spear pointed at him with bored conceit.

'I will join you shortly. We need to get those shackles off first.'

'Are you sure you will be safe with him?' asked Gunnar quietly. But Hakon must have heard him because his blue gaze swept over to them with predatory swiftness.

'I gave my word and I will honour it. I will be her protector from now until my final breath,' he said.

Orla stared at him in shock…yes, that was what she had made him agree to, but to hear it said seemed strange, even to her own ears. The sheer certainty in his voice sent a shiver down her spine.

Had she bound herself to this man forever?

He didn't look happy about it—in fact, he looked slightly disgusted.

Well, if he was a jarl, marrying a simple farmer would be a steep step down for him.

Gunnar focused on untying the women, obviously happy to leave her with him now that he had openly sworn his allegiance. 'Be sure to make it public, Mistress. The sooner the news spreads of your new husband, the better. Hopefully our tormentors will think twice before attacking again,' he said, before leading the women away.

'Tormentors?' Hakon asked, taking a step forward, the spear still following him.

'He is mine. You can go,' she said to the spear-bearer, who grumbled about the ingratitude of stupid women as he left.

'Tell me about the attacks. I must know everything if I am to succeed.'

'Hopefully marrying me will be enough to deter them,' she said curtly, turning away.

He didn't follow.

Sighing at his obstinacy, she grabbed him by the metal around his wrists and tugged him forward. 'This summer I have had ten sheep disappear. At first, we thought they had merely got lost, but there has been no sign of them, they simply vanished…one at a time. I suspect it is a neighbour filling their bellies on our meat. I have gathered the flock into one field, but it is difficult to keep a watch over them.

'Then there was the damage to our barn—someone tried to torch it. But our dogs alerted us and we were able to stop the fire quickly.'

They had reached the blacksmith by then and she called out to the man working the forge, 'Can you take these chains off? You can keep the iron.'

The blacksmith looked at Orla with concern. 'Are you sure you want me to?' he asked, adding softly with concern a moment later, 'This isn't the…usual kind of thrall you buy. Where is Gunnar?'

She had always liked the blacksmith, so she didn't take offence to his question. 'Oh, he is not a thrall. He is my new husband. Hakon Eriksson.'

The blacksmith's wife darted out from the workshop as if her skirts were on fire. 'Did you say *husband*? Mistress Orla, have you really bought a thrall to be your husband?' The couple exchanged horrified looks.

'Yes.' Orla nodded. 'As soon as he is free of these chains, we will do a simple handfasting and then return to my farm. Skalla kept saying I needed a husband… Well, I have bought myself one and I think him quite fine. Do you not agree?' Orla asked with a wide grin, as she slapped at the muscle on Hakon's arm.

He stared down at her as if she were mad, but she ignored him.

The blacksmith's wife's mouth dropped open, but she nodded dumbly. 'He is certainly…*big*.'

'Exactly!' Orla declared proudly, the idea of her new protector growing on her with every passing moment.

'He was a…' She paused. Should she say that he was a jarl or would people look down on him for losing his jarldom? 'A mighty warrior…until he was betrayed. I took one look at him and knew he was the perfect man for me! A handsome and impressive catch—straight off the boat. Fortune favours me, do you not think?'

Hakon shrugged off her touch and stepped forward, holding out his wrists for the blacksmith, who immediately went to work unchaining him. 'I am a jarl,' he said firmly, daring Orla to contradict him with one heavy look.

'Not any more,' she mumbled and his eyes narrowed.

Chapter Four

Hakon tried not to let her words unsettle him. She hadn't said them unkindly—her tone had been gentle, pitying almost. Somehow that felt worse, as if he were a child, unaware of life's cruelties.

Maybe he was?

He had fought in wars, suffered injury and defeat. But he had never truly known what it was to be denied his freedom. Until now.

But did she really have to point it out so bluntly?

Could he not keep one scrap of his pride in this spiralling fall of dignity? Not only had he lost his power, land and potentially his brothers, too, but he had now given his word to marry and protect a stranger!

What was wrong with her that she needed to buy herself a husband? Surely any man would gladly step forward to protect her.

Was she mad?

She did appear a little strange. Ridiculously jubilant considering she was wedding herself to a man in chains.

But he realised she was also honest and compassionate, after her speech to Mildritha and Wynflaed. He was still surprised she had freed them immediately. Anyone else would have seen his affection towards them and would have used their presence to wield greater power over him. Orla had done the opposite.

Apparently, it was something she routinely did. It made him feel guilty that he had never thought to do something similar with his own thralls. He treated his people well, had never been a cruel master, but then, the hierarchy of people had been written in the sagas. There were thralls, karls, jarls and kings and your birth dictated where you were placed. If you rose or fell, it was because of the will of the gods and the weavings of fate. He had never thought to question it.

Not until he had lost his own freedom.

The shackles were broken, and the chains dropped into a bucket with a rusty clang. He imagined they would be reworked into something new, a tool, perhaps, or a bridle. He hoped they would be anything but chains. He hated them and had bloody sores and blisters around his ankles and wrists from wearing them. But it was the humiliation of wearing them that had hurt the most.

'Better?' Orla asked, with a bright smile, and he nodded, absently rubbing his wrists to soothe the ache of them.

'Thank you.' It seemed a poor response after she had paid for his freedom, but then again, she had not done it solely out of kindness. As she had said to the two sisters, all freedom came at a cost: they were bound to her for at least a year and he was to be her husband—a much greater price.

Fate was a twisted serpent.

A feisty, red-headed Celt was the last woman Hakon would have ever imagined as his bride.

But he could not claim to be angered by it. Frustrated by the circumstances, yes, but angry? No.

He would make short work of destroying her enemies. That way he could leave as early as the start of the next sailing season. Even though waiting until spring wasn't ideal, it was still quicker than if he'd had to regain his freedom alone. Escaping or earning passage back to Norway could have taken years and that was what Ingvar was counting on.

Orla's brisk tone brought him back to the present. 'Let's go to the wise man *gothi*, perform our marriage ceremony, and then we can set off home before it gets dark.' As she spoke, she wrapped her arm around his, not caring that he was practically naked beside her, leading him cheerfully away from the smithy as if they were a couple in love.

When he stared at the familiarity of her touch, she rolled her eyes at him as if he really were dim-witted. 'I want no one to doubt our relationship. I have many enemies, remember, and not all are known to me.'

That caught his attention and he began to scan the market square for any signs of malcontent. Several people stared at them, some of them with obvious disgust—the man called Snorri was one of them.

She leaned a little closer to him then, as if they were conspirators in this plot. 'The blacksmith's wife will do most of our work for us. She is a terrible gossip… I should have asked before, but are you already married?'

She asked the question lightly, as if she did not care about the answer, and that surprised him.

'It matters not if you are. Many men in Iceland have wives back in their homeland. When they don't return, it is presumed their wives will divorce them in their absence. I am sure they would not mind you marrying for the sake of your freedom, especially as I will never have reason or opportunity to make a claim on your estate,' she said thoughtfully, as they made their way towards the wise man *gothi*'s house and temple.

Odin's teeth, she spoke incessantly!

'I have no wife.'

Yet.

'Really?' she exclaimed. 'I would have thought a man like you would have been betrothed at a young age…or so I have heard.'

She blushed a little and he wondered if she really did think him a handsome and impressive match, as she had said to the blacksmith and his wife. Quickly he dismissed it. She had been speaking of his status, that was all.

'I was betrothed, twice.'

'Twice betrothed, but never married?'

He sighed, a little annoyed that she had somehow cut deep into the heart of one of his greatest failures. 'The first died before reaching maturity. The second refused me.' At her look of surprised concern, he quickly added, 'She fell in love with a friend of mine. I was happy for them. But, yes, I am still unmarried which is unusual for a man of my age and position.'

They were in front of the wise man *gothi*'s temple now and Orla looked up at him with a lopsided smile. 'It sounds as if you have been unlucky in love. I am sorry this marriage will not be any better for you. Some things are just not meant to be.'

Gentle green eyes met his own and they were filled with sympathy. But with a determined clench of her jaw, she turned away before he could respond and called out for the Norse priest *gothi*, 'Come quickly, we wish to be married!'

Orla had requested a simple handfasting ceremony, in the middle of the square. People solemnly gathered around to witness it.

Before he began, the priest *gothi*—a tiny old man who resembled a mole—asked Orla repeatedly if she wished to delay the ceremony.

'At least until you have taken time to…consider your choices,' he said, squinting up at them and then glancing hopelessly around the crowd, as if hoping someone would step up to agree with him.

By the worried looks of those around them, Hakon would guess they were thinking much the same as the priest *gothi*, and that his marriage to Orla was far more significant than he had originally thought.

Was she an important landholder?

It seemed unusual for a Celtic woman, who by her own admission had once been a slave herself, to be such a significant person in Iceland.

'I am certain,' replied Orla, who was relentlessly positive about the whole thing, which seemed strange to him. He could understand his own motives for marrying a stranger, but hers seemed ridiculous in comparison.

Surely any man here would happily marry her instead, especially if she was an important landowner? Hakon suspected the answer lay in the enemies she had mentioned.

Words were spoken, although he barely heard them, his attention transfixed by the bright and eager smiles of his bride, who seemed almost gleeful when the cords of marriage were wrapped around their hands and their marriage declared.

The ceremony was complete, but there were no cheers or well wishes at the end.

Orla waved happily to the crowd as they left, untroubled by the fact that she had bound herself to a stranger.

'Why are you so damn cheerful?' he eventually asked, as he led her begrudgingly by the arm out of the square.

She glanced up at him, the sunny smile not even faltering. 'You are not the only person to buy their freedom with this marriage.'

'Surely you could have your pick of men… Why me?'

'Because you are perfect…' she grinned '…and you will not stay.'

'Explain,' he growled between gritted teeth.

Orla shrugged. 'I am the heir to a large plot of land and a prosperous farm. But I am not Norse. My father bought and adopted me as a child.'

'He adopted a thrall?' He had never heard of such

a thing, but then Iceland was so remote, he supposed they lived by their own laws.

'Yes. But my father's brother, and possibly others, have coveted my inheritance. They wish for me to marry my uncle's son…but only so that they can control me. I fear I will not live long, even if I do as they say. They do not view me as their kin.'

He opened his mouth to ask another question, but as they neared the cart that held Gunnar and the two Saxon sisters there was a sudden commotion behind them. Hakon turned, instinctively shielding and pushing Orla behind him. A man dressed in a wealthy tunic strode towards them, his guards pushing the crowd aside to make way for him.

'Orla, what is the meaning of this?' barked the man. He had blue eyes and long, dark hair neatly braided down his back. His beard was equally well kept, and he wore plenty of bronze, silver and gold to suggest he was a man of significant standing on the island.

'Cousin Njal! How lovely to see you on such a happy day.' Orla beamed at the man with a smile that seemed almost insulting in its smugness.

Her clever eyes slid towards Hakon with a pointed look, as if to say, *This is the man they wish me to marry.*

'Happy?' blustered Njal. 'What have you done now, you obstinate woman? They say you are married now and to a thrall no less! I should have known dirt would seek out dirt!'

Not liking Njal's rough and offensive words, Hakon took a step forward. 'She has married me. My name is Hakon Eriksson and I am a Norwegian jarl—King Harald's trusted man. Speak with me if you wish to discuss it further, although I suggest you use a more respectful tone first!'

Njal's face turned purple as he choked on his outrage. 'You think I care who you are? Norwegian jarls have no place here! We are far from King Harald's rule and we prefer it that way. My father is an important *godi* of this island and is Orla's guardian—you cannot marry her without his permission.'

Orla flushed with anger and she stepped around Hakon. 'I am not a child! My father gave me permission to pick anyone of my choosing. Skalla asked me to marry quickly and I have!'

Njal took another step forward, glaring down at Orla, his fists clenched. 'You *know* what was expected of you.' He raised his hand as if to slap her, and Orla flinched. 'You stupid b—!'

Njal's eyes bulged as Hakon's hand snapped out to grip him by the throat. Hakon moved forward, blocking Orla once more with his body. 'As you are *family*, I will not kill you this time. But if you dare raise your hand to her, or speak to my wife again with disrespect, then I will rip out your throat.'

Njal beat his fists against Hakon's arms. When that did not work, he tried clawing at the already broken skin of his wrists. Hakon was too filled with anger to notice the pain—he squeezed until the man's eyes began to roll back.

Njal's guards unsheathed their swords, but seemed uncertain about what to do. With his free hand Hakon took the sword at Njal's belt and then released him with a sharp push.

Njal dropped like a stone in the mud and his guards took a hesitant step forward.

If anything, their indecision only enraged Hakon further and he pointed his sword at them with a snarl. 'In Norway, no one would insult or attack another man's wife! Is this land lawless? Is there no decency here? Attack me if you wish. I will kill you all without a moment's hesitation.' He twisted the sword with a flourish, demonstrating his speed and skill, before lowering it slightly into a resting position.

The crowd filled with murmurs, although whether it was with approval or not, he couldn't be certain. The guards took a hesitant step back, lowering their weapons.

'A wise decision,' Hakon said and noticed how the crowd neither helped nor rebuked Njal and his guards.

Understanding washed through him like a cold wind. Orla was fighting alone. No one here had the confidence to step forward and protect a lone woman against men like Skalla and Njal. They were too cowardly to stand up for what was just and honourable. Too far removed from the rest of the world to obey the laws of decency.

Well, that would end, *now.*

With disgust he crouched down to look Njal firmly in his red, raw eyes. 'Farewell…*cousin.*'

Chapter Five

Hakon turned from the men as if he knew they had no courage and strode away, leading Orla by the elbow to the cart. She had to hurry her steps to keep up with him. When she glanced behind her, she saw the group of men, including Njal, looked as dumbfounded by his behaviour as she was.

She looked up at Hakon with greater respect. His courage and strength had been awe-inspiring and Orla would be lying if she said she hadn't been a little thrilled by his actions. No one, apart from Oddr, had ever protected or stood up for her like that and it felt...*good*.

It was foolish, of course, and could easily lead to more trouble in the future. But she had to admit, it felt wonderful to have someone on *her* side for a change.

'Get in and let us be gone...before they change their minds,' he whispered and she hurried to do as he said, fear speeding her actions.

Gunnar dropped down from his driving seat and handed Hakon the reins. 'Here you go, Master, the

horse knows the way. You need only urge it to walk…
or run…possibly.'

As her old friend passed her to get in the back of the
cart with the women, he muttered, 'Well, you have certainly awoken a bear. Let us hope he does not devour
us, too.'

Orla climbed up and sat beside Hakon, glancing awkwardly at Njal's sword which lay in front of their feet.
She swallowed nervously, glancing up at the powerful
man who had moments before almost killed her cousin
with his bare hands.

As he cracked the reins and moved them forward,
she noticed the blood trickling down his arms. Stoop-
ing down, she reached for the hem of her shift, ready
to tear off strips to bandage him with.

'Don't,' he said firmly.

'But you're bleeding, I should bandage your wounds
at least.'

'Take these.' He handed her the reins. He reached
down and ripped strips off the bottom of his trousers.

'But the cloth is dirty!'

'They are only small flesh wounds.'

Pity swelled in her heart as she looked more carefully at the other wounds on his body. Red raw slashes
across his back from a whip and horrible purple bruises
around his ribs. All of which was startling, but the
sheer breadth and strength of his muscular body so
close to hers affected her strangely. Her mouth became
dry and she couldn't seem to look away from the way
his arms and chest rippled as he moved.

'What? You wanted me to bind them,' he said, raising a dark blond brow at her in question.

Gulping deeply, she forced her eyes back to the muddy road and flicked the reins to encourage the horse to go faster. 'A dirty cloth could do more damage than good,' she said, scrabbling for an excuse as to why she was staring at him for so long.

'It will do, until you can tend to them properly.'

He took the reins from her. 'Tell me about your uncle and cousin. Everything.'

So, Orla did. She explained how she had inherited her land. How her uncle and cousin could not openly go against her father's wishes, but that they had pressured her to marry, taken labourers and votes in the assembly from her, and used her hay fields without permission. That she wasn't sure who supported her, that her sheep were going missing and it could be Snorri, her uncle or any of her neighbours taking advantage of her position.

When she was done, he asked more questions, wanting to know everything from the number of men bound to Skalla to the names and details of her neighbours. He paid particular attention to men like Snorri and asked similar questions about their strength and power of influence.

It took until they arrived back at the farm for her to be done speaking. Her people began to emerge from the barns and longhouse to greet them. Everyone else began to get out of the cart, but Hakon remained where he was and examined everyone with interest.

'So many women,' he said, his voice hard and filled with disapproval.

Orla bristled at the censure in his tone, but then she could understand his dismay—they were no match against her uncle. 'Skalla took many of the male labourers with him. He offered them their own land to farm and they couldn't resist the offer. I would not change how I run things here, but I guess that is the problem with having no thralls—they are free to leave as they wish.'

'How many did he take?'

She cringed. 'Five. I didn't have that many men to start with.'

His blue eyes pivoted towards her, sharp as a blade. 'Five? I can count only three men here and a handful of boys. Why do these remain—are they sons or husbands of your bondswomen?'

She nodded, hating that he had guessed it so easily. 'Except Gunnar…' Gunnar walked past them, his old body limping heavily as he guided the two sisters to the longhouse.

Hakon gave her a heavy look, before asking, 'And, when do those bondswomen earn their freedom? How long are they and their men likely to stay with you?'

'Until spring…although, most say they will stay after.'

Hakon spat out a curse before saying, 'Until they are offered better!' He rose from his seat quickly, causing her to jump. The sudden movement caught his eye and he looked down at her with a wrinkled brow. 'Are you afraid of me?'

Tilting her chin defiantly, she asked, 'Should I be?' She almost laughed at her own stupidity. She had picked

Hakon because he was a warrior, but in truth she hadn't thought about what he would have to do to *prove* himself to Skall and Njal. Now she had seen first-hand what a powerful man was capable of and it had unsettled her.

Had she really invited a bear into her home?

'I do not hurt women or children,' he said dismissively, leaping down into the mud with a heavy squelch.

Orla stared at his bare feet and hurried down to join him, passing the reins to one of the boys who took care of the animals. 'Come, you should bathe and dress in fresh clothes.'

'Thank you, *Wife*,' he replied and she tried to ignore the shiver that ran down her spine. It felt as if he had claimed and branded her with that simple title. She had been a slave, a daughter and a landowner, but nothing felt more intimate than wife.

As Hakon thudded into the longhouse, he wondered if fighting a bear unarmed or ploughing a hundred fields would be preferable to the current political mess he found himself in.

At least he knew the truth. He would need an army, or the support of his neighbours, to overcome Skalla and Njal. The only thing holding them back was the obvious wishes of her father, so maybe there was some decency left in people, even this far from the rest of the world. He would need to play on that strength, become as valued in the community as Oddr had been.

It would be difficult, but Hakon was a jarl. He knew how to appeal to the hearts of neighbours and build strong alliances. It could be done and a part of him loved the challenge of it, although returning to his brothers was still the most important of his goals.

Orla's hall was impressive. She had spoken of her land as a prosperous farm, but her longhouse was as big as his own back home.

It was almost the length of a field and as wide as three or four hay carts. The walls were built of thick stone and turf, with wooden panelling on the inside to keep back the soil. The roof was made of timber, but was also covered with turf to trap in heat.

Inside it was darker than his home back in Norway, but he imagined the winters were harsher here, and the stone-turf structure would be warmer, as well as use less wood. There were fewer trees in Iceland and he had heard they sometimes imported wood for their buildings, so it made sense.

The elaborately carved and painted doors were left wide open, as it was the end of summer. The smoke-hole covers had been removed in the ceiling above to allow in as much light as possible and, combined with the light from the central fire and torches, the room glowed with welcome.

After the storage rooms was the main chamber, with a narrow fire trough running down its centre. Several looms were positioned either side of it, far more than was normal, as well as huge piles of fleeces and large platforms presumably for either storage or areas for combing out the fleeces. Drop spindles and all manner of spinning and weaving tools were neatly stored in baskets everywhere.

The quantity produced must be incredible and he

had a feeling this was the real reason why Orla's property was so coveted and was also why they had not yet been openly attacked. It would make no sense to destroy the very thing you wanted.

After the wool production area there were several wide benches, tables and chests running either side of the firepit. Presumably, living and sleeping areas for all the many women and children that lived here. No weapons or shields decorated the walls at all and that was worrying, but not totally unexpected.

I could take this sword and leave. Who would stop me?

Shaking his head, he sucked in another deep breath and tried to think of a more honourable plan, one that would save Orla's home.

'Welcome, come in!' said Orla with a wide sweep of her hand, gesturing him towards the back of the hall. 'We are so glad to have you with us, Hakon! All will be well now!'

Hakon grimaced at the naive assumption. 'I think that is being too optimistic. We could face an open attack any day.'

'But why?' She shook her head, obviously horrified by the thought. 'They have no reason to, I hold no grudges with anyone. Even Skalla has no reason to hate me and I am married now. I have a warrior husband who can cast my vote in the assembly and who can demand Skalla give me my hay. I am sure they will be annoyed for a time, but they will have to learn to accept it eventually.'

Hakon almost stopped to beat his head against the

wall. 'You think they need a reason? You are weak, surrounded by mostly women and children without weapons or warriors. Did you really think marrying one man would be enough to protect you?'

Chapter Six

Orla glanced around her at the worried expressions of her people. She grabbed his arm and hurried him towards the back of the hall, calling back to her women as she walked, 'Please can you bring my husband some fresh clothing? Some of those winter yule gifts we made for our neighbours should work for now. We will be in our chamber…where we can discuss all possibilities… even the *unlikely ones*…' She glared meaningfully at him with her last words.

Hakon followed her willingly. He could understand her not wanting to alarm anyone, but frankly, they needed to be ready for all possibilities, *especially* attack.

Orla's private chambers were large and divided into sections by timber-framed screens covered with elaborately decorated tapestries. The first chamber seemed more like a guest chamber, with a large wooden bed pushed to the side and lots of chairs and chests arranged around a brazier. Beyond was the master's bedchamber—which was probably her father's until he died. In it he could see a very large bed box, with another brazier and some storage chests in front of it.

'Are you mad?' she snapped, turning on him with narrowed eyes. 'They are frightened enough as it is without you adding to their fears!'

Ah, so she hoped to reassure them by feeding them false promises.

'Should I lie, pretend that all is well? I will not do that—they need to prepare themselves for the worst!' He sighed. 'Honestly, I am not sure what I can do to help you. I am only one man!'

Orla glared back at him. 'You are enough. I need a husband only to protect my claim. I have the respect and loyalty of many families. Skalla cannot take from me without losing his influence, because he swore openly to honour and protect my inheritance. You saw how angry Njal was. They can do nothing to me now that I am married, not openly at least.'

'That may change now that you are married. It may give him an excuse to act.' Hakon sat heavily in one of the chairs, and scratched his itchy beard. He could not wait to remove the dirt and grime from it. Irritated, he snapped, 'I saw how much you paid for me. I have spent double that on a new cloak, yet this *marriage* may cost me my life!'

She folded her hands across her chest. 'You agreed to the bargain.'

Closing his eyes, he nodded wearily. 'I did. I am tired…it has been a long day.'

A soft hand covered his own. Startled, he opened his eyes to see Orla looking down at him with sympathetic and remorseful eyes. 'I am sorry. You have been through so much and I have not helped matters. You will feel much better after a hot bath and some decent food.'

Several women entered the room and her hand flew away. They placed a bundle of clothing wrapped in linen on the table before hurrying from the room.

Orla waited until they had gone before speaking. 'You should also remember that you are a *jarl*.'

'You believe me, then?'

She rolled her eyes. 'No one but a jarl would antagonise a group of armed men so casually. Now, listen! People here act as if they do not care about King Harald or his nobility, but that is not true. They fear it. They are all *terrified* that he might come here one day and claim this island as his own. Strip them of everything they have worked so hard for. Your presence will intimidate them and they will wish to make alliances with you, ensuring they have the ear of the King on their side… if such a thing were to happen.'

Hakon scoffed, 'Harald has enough problems within his own lands. He does not care about a miserable rock at the very edge of the world.'

Orla's lips tightened and he realised he had offended her. 'That may be so, but old fears are hard to shake. Now that I have a husband, I can regain my vote at the assembly… You need only name Gunnar as your proxy vote before you leave. He is loyal to me and then I can have a say in our laws, hire men, buy weapons…'

'Skalla stopped you from hiring men?'

She nodded. 'Yes, he has been slowly bleeding us of

our strength. As a maiden, I was seen as too vulnerable to look after myself. But now that I have a husband, he can no longer order me around, or forbid others from working with me. Even if you leave and rarely return, I still have more power as a wife than I did as a maiden under his guardianship. It is stupid, but it is the way of things.'

Hakon nodded—Norway was not much different. Women could have power as wives or widows, but maidens had none. It was presumed that girls would be protected by their families, until they ran one of their own. He had never thought of it as unfair, but then the last few weeks had taught him a lot about the injustices in the world.

Orla continued to speak, her earlier offer of a hot bath apparently forgotten. 'Skalla was once reasonable. He will have to accept that I am married now and forget his plans to combine my land with his.'

'You think it will be that easy?' he asked, staring at her and trying to decide whether she was being deliberately naive or simply had no sense to start with.

She placed her hands on her hips and gave a disgruntled huff. 'What is the alternative? Should I have married Njal instead? If so, Snorri's bear would be cutting his teeth on your bones before nightfall.'

'True... Now, are you ever going to order me that bath?' he teased, enjoying the way her cheeks heated as she realised her mistake.

'Of course!' She picked up the bundle of clothing and pushed it into his hands. 'Follow me,' she said curtly, grabbing a basket of supplies and marching into the chamber beyond.

To his surprise, they passed through her bedchamber and walked towards a screened-off area at the back of the room.

Unable to help himself, he glanced curiously at the bed box as they passed.

It was built for warmth, raised up from the floor, and enclosed on three sides with wooden panelling. The open side was shielded by a heavy woollen curtain that ran over the top of the large frame.

Would they sleep together in it?

Probably not, they were strangers, and this had been an alliance formed for their mutual gain…not a true marriage.

On the wall beside it was a large round shield and battle-axe. Hakon smiled, relieved at the sight of decent weaponry. He would not have to rely on Njal's badly balanced sword after all.

Orla cleared her throat, drawing his attention back to her. She was blushing fiercely and he realised he had been grinning at the bed like an idiot.

He cleared his own throat awkwardly. 'The shield and axe… I am glad to see it.'

'They were my father's, but you may have them. They are no use to me,' she said primly, then slipped behind the screen.

There was the scrape of metal on wood and, when Hakon joined her, he realised there was a bolted door at the back of the room. It was an unexpected sight, as the hall had been built jutting out of the hillside.

Surely there would be nothing at the back but earth?

The door swung open to reveal a dark tunnel and Orla took a moment to take a torch from the wall sconce and light it with a flintstone hanging from her belt. 'This tunnel leads to a hot pool and stream on the other side of the hill. My father dug this tunnel so that we could bathe in it even in the middle of winter.'

Hakon followed her inside. The tunnel was supported with stone and wood, and was surprisingly clean considering the fact they were walking beneath a hill.

'I heard this land spat fire and ice…'

She laughed. 'It does! Although the pool I am taking you to is very pleasant, and not too hot. You should be careful of the pools further north…some of those can cook meat faster than fire. You would not wish to fall into one of those.'

He grimaced. 'I can't imagine anything worse!'

Orla chuckled. 'Once Snorri got drunk and fell into a geyser. He says he was shot into the air a hundred feet… But I doubt it…fifty maybe.'

The tunnel widened out and he found himself in a little hut, with benches and pegs for bathing. He was still only wearing his torn trousers, but he didn't feel cold. The wooden floor beneath his toes was warm and dry. He felt the layers of mud begin to flake off his skin as heat seeped up through the soles of his feet.

Opening the door to the hut, Orla lit a brazier and then extinguished her torch, placing it in a waiting wall sconce. 'We exchange them each time,' she explained, pointing to the other, 'so be sure to bring the right one back.'

Placing the linen bundle on the bench, he followed her outside. A lightly steaming pool lined with flat stones was waiting only a few feet away from the opening. The water appeared to spring up from a fountain to the side and poured from the pool in a little stream down the hillside.

Orla placed the basket of supplies at the edge of the water. 'Don't worry about the faint smell, it's clean. There is soap, wash-cloths and bandages here for you. *Nattmal* will be served soon, so be quick.' Then she walked back towards him and the shelter.

It was the first time he had been left alone in weeks and for some reason his heart began to race. He reached out and grabbed her hand, enjoying the feel of her silky skin in the centre of his coarse palm. 'You won't be joining me…*Wife*?'

A wicked part of him hoped to see that rosy blush from earlier on her cheeks once more. Immediately he regretted his teasing because she stopped dead in front of him and stared up at him for a moment, as if she were trying to determine whether he meant it or not. Hakon had never been good at jests; he was too serious most of the time for them to fall right.

'You expect this to be a real marriage?'

Odin's teeth!

He wasn't sure what to say. He found her attractive and, unlike his last two brides-to-be, Orla had at least *wanted* to marry him.

He wanted her. There was no denying it. But would it be wise, if he was going to leave her anyway? Then again, she *was* his wife.

What did it matter if she lived across the ocean?

His own parents had lived such separate lives they might as well have been divided by a sea.

'Only if you wish it.' He reached out to cup her face gently and stroked his thumb down her flushed cheek, the heat of her skin warming his thumb.

Green eyes that matched the rolling hills widened. 'I will think about it,' she answered, her tone almost cold with its impartiality, as if she were considering whether to eat mutton or fish for her evening meal.

'You will?' he asked, a little shocked that his casual teasing had borne unexpected fruit.

Dipping his head until there was only a whisper of opportunity between them, he waited for her to step back, to reject him and scurry away like a frightened rabbit.

She didn't move and his heart began to hammer in his chest. Copper eyelashes fluttered down to hide her eyes and her head tilted ever so slightly towards him like a gift.

Closing the distance slowly, he gently brushed his mouth against her lips. They felt soft and willing, the tenderest of caresses. Lust struck like lightning and he wondered what else she might allow. Sweeping his free arm around her waist, he pulled her against him, gripping her face more firmly with his hand as he deepened the kiss.

Hesitant hands reached up to lie flat against his naked chest and he allowed the growing temptation to consume him, stroking his tongue lightly between her lips, before brushing his mouth a second time against hers. She gasped lightly, opening more for him as he pressed harder against her. The rigid length of him pressed against her belly and he stifled a moan at the sudden strength of his arousal.

This was not what he had intended, but he could not help himself.

Her eyes opened and her palms pushed him gently away. The kiss was broken and they were left breathless and shocked.

'We will speak later,' she said, then left him.

Chapter Seven

Hakon left the pool feeling refreshed and surprisingly optimistic.

No wonder Orla was so cheerful about life, with such a luxury only a short walk from her bed.

The weeks of his gruelling enslavement had been washed away by the soothing lap of heated water on his skin. He had even fallen asleep at one point, sitting on a small shelf within the pool, waking to see the sun lower in the sky. He hadn't slept for long, but it had been enough to restore him.

He had washed his hair and tied it back with a strip from one of the bandages. His beard had been so badly matted in places that he was forced to crop it short with the grooming shears he had found.

The basket was filled with all manner of combs, shears and soaps, as well as healing salves which he slathered on to his wounds before bandaging them. The tunic was simple compared to what he had worn as a jarl, but it was well made and broad enough in the shoulders to fit him.

The trousers were loose around the waist and a little short in the leg. They revealed the bandages around his ankles when he walked. The boots would fit with a little stretching—a little rubbing of his toes felt like a small price to pay to protect his feet. Several times during the journey he had been afraid he would lose one or two of his toes. The sea air was harsh and no matter how much water was bailed there was always some in the bottom of the boat. He had rowed every day with his feet in cold water.

Thankfully, all of his toes had survived the journey. He hoped the same could be said for his brothers. For some reason, he was beginning to believe they had.

Possibly it was Orla's influence. She had made him think about what it was to be lucky and he had to admit that fortune *had* favoured him, despite Ingvar's betrayal.

He could have died in his bed, but some noise had woken him. Then, he had managed to help both his brothers escape, without being killed himself—which was incredible! Even when Hakon had been sold into slavery and cast out to the furthest corner of the world, he had still managed to end up free and in a position of power within the first day of landing here.

Tenuous power, he reminded himself, before Orla's positivity blinded him completely to the facts.

He would need to work quickly to secure Orla's land and influence, so that he could return home, liberate his brothers from false accusations and seek vengeance against Ingvar.

Despite the challenges ahead, Hakon had to admit

that it was no longer just his word that made him act as her sword and shield. He had grown to like and admire her in only a short time. Her generous and tenacious spirit appealed to him and when Njal had raised his hand to her…he had genuinely wanted to kill the man.

As he made his way back through the tunnel, he thought about their kiss. It burned far brighter than any other he had had before.

Why was that? And why had he suggested their marriage be real?

It would never work. Eventually, he would return to Norway and he doubted Orla would ever willingly leave her home.

Still, fate had bound them together and he was beginning to think he should not question it. Allow the gods to decide, as they had not failed him yet…

Not really.

Besides, a marriage was only meant for the creation of children. She might want a child to inherit her farm and he did not need one. When each of his betrothals had failed, he had decided to name Grimr his heir instead.

When he entered the bedchamber and rebolted the door, he heard an unfamiliar voice coming from the hall. The man didn't sound angry, but Hakon would not take an unnecessary risk. Without hesitation, he took the axe and shield from the wall and carried them to the door. He placed them within easy reach before stepping out to meet his unwelcome guest.

A man with grey hair and a bulky figure sat sprawled in the guest of honour's chair. He bore a striking resemblance to Njal, although this man, despite his more advanced years, seemed sharper and in better control of his emotions then Njal. If anything, that worried Hakon more. Orla was pouring him a horn of ale and the women were scurrying hastily to fill the table with the *nattmal* meal.

The man's eyes slid towards him and narrowed with obvious malcontent. 'You must be Hakon. I heard you attacked my son today. I want an apology and the return of my family's sword.'

Orla's eyes met his and he could tell, without her speaking a word, that she was afraid.

Orla's chest tightened as she waited for Hakon to speak. He stood in the doorway of her chambers, looking more breathtakingly handsome than she could have ever imagined, and she had thought him good-looking before his bath.

It was a pity Skalla was here to ruin everything. She had forgotten about the stolen sword and now she was afraid it would be his perfect excuse.

'I was explaining—' she said, but Hakon interrupted her.

'There is no need.' He moved with the ease of a predatory wolf and came to stand beside her, offering her a chair.

She took it, helpless to do anything more, and Hakon sat beside her, taking the jug from her hand and filling himself a horn of ale.

'No need?' asked Skalla, with a calmness that made her nervous.

Njal was like a boar, all clumsy bluster and rage. He could be difficult to handle if provoked, which was precisely why she usually avoided him. But Skalla could never be avoided—he was like a snake, slithering in whenever he was least wanted and striking with unexpected accuracy and speed.

She had not expected him to come here, had hoped that Njal would be too humiliated to mention the attack, or that Skalla would not have taken insult at his son's recklessness. But he had arrived, alone and without guards, demanding an apology and the return of his property. It was a deliberate move, she realised, the first step in a war she had assumed could never happen. Now, she was beginning to fear she had only made the situation worse by marrying a stranger.

Hakon rolled the ale in his cup and took a long sip. 'It has been many weeks since I last tasted ale.' He smiled at Orla. 'It is delicious.'

She gave a weak nod of thanks, glancing at Skalla, who watched Hakon with growing resentment.

'You owe me an apology, boy!'

'My name is Jarl Hakon Eriksson,' Hakon returned. 'And why should I apologise? For taking the sword? It was such poor workmanship I did not think it had any real value. If you want it, we can return it gladly. Is it still in the cart?' he asked Orla.

Swallowing the knot in her throat, she answered, 'I have asked Gunnar to get it.'

Hakon smiled warmly at her and some of her nervousness dissipated. 'Good.' He took a bread trencher from the pile and began heaping stew on to it.

'You tried to kill my son!' Skalla slammed his fist down on the table, his voice smacking against the walls like a whip.

Orla jumped in her seat and Hakon reached beneath the table and squeezed her thigh gently, before releasing it and reaching for his horn. 'Your son raised his hand against my wife.' He took a sip, swallowing it leisurely before turning back to Skalla. 'As you are family, I decided against killing him today…out of respect.'

Skalla's lip curled. *'Family.'* He leaned forward to glare at Orla. 'You married without my permission.'

'He is a jarl,' Orla replied tartly. 'Why would I need permission to marry a jarl? Such a connection can only benefit myself and the island.'

Hakon smiled and she wondered if it was because he had noticed her failure to say that it would benefit Skalla.

'*If* he is a jarl… He arrived in chains.'

'I did… But I give you my word, I am a jarl,' Hakon said, digging into his meal. She knew the mutton was deliciously rich and she wasn't surprised he would enjoy it after so many weeks of deprivation. But still, his lack of concern was off-putting, even to her.

'Then you will not be staying for long?'

'Long enough… I have two brothers. They also like to travel.'

The implication was clear. Orla would remain protected, even in his absence. She breathed a sigh of relief.

Skalla began to drink his ale thoughtfully, the previous anger pulled back and tightly restrained. 'Are you sure you want this, Orla? To trust your safety with a man you barely know? There is still time to break this... I can arrange a match for you. One that will make you happy.'

As he spoke, Hakon ate his meal greedily, barely looking up as he spooned the stew into his mouth, as if he found their conversation tiresome.

Orla felt as if a hundred spiders were climbing across her skin—she couldn't understand how Hakon could be so relaxed. But she rallied some courage and replied coldly, 'To Njal? No, thank you.'

Skalla tilted his head as if acknowledging her displeasure. 'I had hoped you would choose Njal of your own accord, but I see now that you are not suited to one another. Your Celtic temper is too...*stubborn.*'

The last word was filled with disapproval and Hakon put down his spoon with a thud.

Then he began to tear at the bread trencher, popping pieces of stew-soaked bread into his mouth and chewing them thoughtfully.

Skalla continued—worryingly, he had the look of a sly merchant about him—'I spoke with some of the men you travelled with, Hakon. They said you were keen to return to Norway. I can organise a ship for you, by tomorrow if you wish. Forget this bargain you have struck with my niece and I will arrange a better match for her. One that suits you both.'

So, that was what he planned: to bribe Hakon into leaving her.

Would he do it?

Her fingers tightened painfully as she gripped the cloth of her skirt beneath the table.

Hakon turned to face her and she had never been so frightened, even when Njal had raised his hand at her. It was nothing to this…this fear that she would be abandoned once again, left alone on unfamiliar shores without anyone to help guide her. He leaned forward, blocking Skalla from her sight, and she gave him the smallest shake of her head, pleading silently with him.

Stay, she mouthed. *Please.*

With a voice as dry as five-day-old bread, Hakon turned back to Skalla and said, 'I have been betrothed twice, but never married. I will not be denied a third wedding night. Besides, I made a promise to Orla and I will keep it. She will be my wife, her lands and people protected by my name until the day I die.'

Orla's shoulders slumped with relief and she tried her best not to cry with relief.

Skalla, however, looked as if he had swallowed a fly. 'Are you sure that is wise? I have heard your jarldom is in a precarious position. You were sold into slavery and, according to the merchant, your brothers retreated from the battle badly wounded. How can you protect Orla if your name is worth nothing?'

Orla feared Hakon would be offended by Skalla's comment, but a slow smile spread across his face and then he gave a deep and unsettling chuckle. 'I am curious… What else did the slaver tell you?'

'No one is questioning your skill as a warrior—I heard how bravely you protected your brothers, allowing them time to escape. You fought fiercely…killing many men with your bare hands like a true berserker. But I fear you will find the life of a farmer dull in comparison—surely you will want to return to Norway as soon as possible to reclaim your power? I can give you silver…to help you regain your title.'

Hakon shrugged lightly, sucking the juice off his long fingers with a relish that made her stomach flip. 'My brothers are still alive, which means Ingvar failed. The power of my jarldom is strong and my brothers will come for me, no doubt after they have punished Ingvar for his stupidity.' He tapered his fingers and leaned back into his seat with a satisfied sigh. 'Do not worry, *Uncle*. My name, and my axe, will be more than enough protection for Orla.'

Gunnar entered the hall, carrying Njal's sword, and Orla broke the tension between the two men by saying, 'The sword is here, Uncle. I am sure you will want to head home after eating. Even though the summer days are long, it will be dark soon. Gunnar, can you prepare Skalla's horse?'

'No need,' snapped Skalla. 'I will stay in your guest chamber tonight…if this is truly what you want, Orla? I mean…you are not a woman normally swayed by passions—at least not with men.'

Heat burned the tips of her ears at Skalla's mocking tone. He was deliberately trying to humiliate and embarrass her, as she was well known for being cold towards men. But it wasn't her fault no one had ever interested her.

Until…Hakon had kissed her. She had been interested then. It was odd that it would be a stranger who would finally be the one to light an interest within her and he definitely had. Their kiss had been overwhelming and not only because it had been her first taste of desire. She suspected it would always be that way with Hakon and no one else could equal him.

It had got her thinking about the reality of their marriage. Why shouldn't it be real? She wanted a child to take over the farm one day and how else would she get an heir? She could not adopt as her father had, that would condemn a child to the same uncertainty she now suffered. But a babe born in marriage…the child of a jarl… Who could argue with that lineage?

The heavy silence grew and Skalla gave a cruel laugh. 'Not that it matters to a man either way.'

She peeked a glance at Hakon and their eyes met. There was a softness to his gaze that she immediately took for pity and her spine stiffened. She refused to be pitied by any man, especially one who owed her thanks for freeing him.

As always, she would take charge of her fate and bend it to her own will.

'You are right. It does not matter,' she agreed coldly. 'But I do look forward to having children. It is what my father would have wanted…for *his grandchildren* to inherit.' Raising her chin, she smiled at Skalla triumphantly. 'I think I will retire for the night. Shall you join me shortly, Husband?'

For the first time Hakon looked uncertain, but to her relief he nodded.

Chapter Eight

Orla quickly stripped down to her shift and climbed into the bed box, firmly drawing the heavy curtain closed and shuffling to the opposite side of the bed. When she had been inspired by the idea of marrying a stranger she had not thought this part through. Skalla's presence only a few feet away would make it even more humiliating, but she would rather face that embarrassment than have any doubt placed upon their marriage.

If she had to be bedded by Hakon within hearing distance of her uncle, then she would accept it. Anything to silence the miserable bastard.

After tonight, Skalla and Hakon could never claim their marriage was a lie and that would protect her in the lonely years to come. Not that she doubted Hakon—at *nattmal* he had been given ample opportunity to abandon her and he hadn't; he had kept his word.

His words circled in her head like a bird of prey. *'I will not be denied a third wedding night.'* Such a statement might have frightened her. But then he had kissed her…

At first his lips had felt as soft and as gentle as a summer breeze, but then it had built quickly into something hotter. A passionate embrace that had promised breathless pleasures. Curious to learn what else he could coax from her body, she was now inclined to grant his small request. After turning down the offer of a ship and silver, she owed him a wedding night at least.

Orla knew what was expected of her; she had asked the women to explain it fully to her when she had first reached marriageable age. Unfortunately, the knowledge had put her off getting married for years. Many of her women's experiences had not been pleasant and, although some had said it *could* be joyous, Orla had not been willing to take the risk.

Kissing Hakon had been nice...better than nice.

So perhaps it wouldn't be so bad. Being rutted like an animal was far from appealing and she certainly hated the idea of a man putting himself inside her, as it sounded hideously uncomfortable. When they had kissed, Hakon's erection had felt large and stiff against her belly—which was worrying. She would have preferred something smaller... Still, maybe it wouldn't last long.

As with all chores, she could not avoid it forever. Marriage would protect her from Skalla and Njal. She could be independent once more, the way she had been when her father was still alive.

Maybe it wouldn't be so bad.

Forcing her mind to focus on better things, she closed her eyes and tried to remember the feel of his kiss. How it had made her breathlessly dizzy with longing and how she had ached for him, her body curving towards him without her realising, until his hard, big body pressed against her and she had wondered what it would be like to be a *real* wife.

You will find out soon enough.

Even if it was awkward and unpleasant, she would do it gladly and hope a child came from their union. It would be worth it to secure her future happiness. There was no point regretting her decision once she had made it.

Skalla had probably hoped to frighten her, speaking about Hakon's capacity for violence. Unfortunately for Skalla, it had done the opposite.

She had learned some things about her new husband that she found strangely comforting. Hakon had fought with savagery, but he had done so to save his brothers, risking his own life to aid their escape. She admired his unwavering loyalty and hoped he would be as brave with the protection of her land and people.

She needed someone powerful and ruthless to keep Skalla in his place and hearing about Hakon's past had convinced her she had made the right choice. Even if he left and never returned, he had promised her men and connections to keep her safe… Maybe she was a fool, but she believed he would keep his promise.

Eventually, the thud of heavy feet made her fingers tighten her grip on the blanket and she lay stiffly, waiting for her husband to arrive. The sounds of clothes being cast aside were like the cracks of a whip in her ears and she swallowed nervously, staring up at the blanketed ceiling.

The wall torches were lit, as well as the brazier, and the summer sun was still pouring in from the smoke hole above. So, she could see reasonably well despite the bed coverings.

The curtain shifted and Hakon slipped under the covers in just his linen braies, the gloriously muscular chest she found so fascinating on full display.

Swallowing nervously, she braced herself for him to turn towards her and begin the act. Maybe he would kiss her first…she hoped he would.

·Silence and her impatience began to grow, until she felt as if she were being suffocated by it. She turned and whispered, 'Should you not begin?'

She could not see his expression clearly, as he was turned away from her, but his tone was clearly confused. 'Begin?'

'Yes!' she hissed. 'Skalla must hear us coupling… or he will claim we are not married.'

Hakon gave a guttural snort of disgust, his voice worryingly loud. 'I do not care what that man thinks.'

'But…'

'No!' he snapped firmly, before closing his eyes.

Horrified, Orla moved closer to his ear so that he could hear her without her having to raise her voice. 'What is *wrong* with you? You were kissing me earlier…' she hissed.

Only heavy silence answered her.

Panic began to claw at her throat and she lay beside him, praying he would change his mind. When he didn't, she decided to take charge of the situation. She would not put her people, land and future at risk because of a *shy* husband!

No, she would convince Skalla this was a true marriage, with or without Hakon's help!

Pushing away the blankets, she knelt beside him on the bed, then pushed her palms against the wooden head of the bed box with all her might. It was old, its joints a little wobbly, and she grinned in the darkness when it shifted with a creak and tapped against the wall. She released it and it made another satisfying sound as it groaned back into place. She pushed again, with firmer resolve this time.

'Odin's teeth, woman. What are you doing—?' Hakon snapped angrily and with her spare hand she instinctively slapped it across his mouth to smother his voice.

'Shh…' she urged, before rocking the bed again, this time throwing her hips forward with her hands to make more of a thud as it hit the wall. She began to rock back and forth in a steady rhythm, although it was hard work with only one hand, and sometimes she missed a beat.

'Stop that!' growled Hakon, pulling her hand away from his mouth.

'Just a little longer,' she whispered slightly out of breath. She increased the pace of her banging in what she hoped would sound like the final thrusts of coupling. The rams were quick, so she imagined men were much the same.

There was a loud bang of a distant door and Orla threw herself across Hakon to peek out of the curtains. 'Has he gone?' she whispered, leaning precariously out to see that the guest bed was indeed empty. 'He has! It worked! He believes our marriage is consummated and has left with his tail between his legs!' she crowed, laughing triumphantly. 'He can't dare question it now.'

She turned to grin at Hakon, who was glaring at her with a thunderous expression, his large torso covered by most of her body and the long fabric of her shift.

'Question what? My ability to hammer my wife like a stubborn nail?' he growled.

Confused by his irritation, she stumbled out of the bed and tied the curtain to the post, so that she could see him better, creating some much-needed distance between them.

'Did I do it for too long? Do you think he will suspect something?' She glanced towards the doorway, half afraid Skalla would return.

Hakon cursed under his breath and looked up at the canopy as if seeking counsel from the gods.

'Will he suspect something?' she repeated, worry making her voice sound almost shrill.

'Only that I am terrible at lovemaking,' he grumbled.

Orla shrugged. 'That does not bother me.'

'It bothers me!' he growled, turning away and slapping his pillow angrily.

Her hands dropped to her hips, as her fear quickly flowed into anger. 'It bothers *me* you did nothing to help! I do not want Skalla to question our marriage after you are gone. He could claim it was all a lie!'

'It *is* a lie!' Hakon barked, sitting up in the bed and glaring at her accusingly.

'It doesn't have to be… You said you would not be denied a third wedding night…'

His brow furrowed as her words sank in, then his expression softened with kindness. 'They were words meant for Skalla… I did not mean for you to take them to heart.'

'You kissed me before,' she accused. 'Have you changed your mind?'

He smiled shyly, glancing away and appearing to struggle to find the right words, before replying, 'No… but I do not want you to feel you have to do something… you do not wish to. I do not care what Skalla thinks or says—'

'But—'

His eyes sharpened and met hers firmly. 'I do not *care* about Skalla. By the time I leave, he will no longer be a problem for you. What you do or don't allow as my wife is separate to him. I only came to your bed tonight to continue the illusion, but I will sleep in your guest chamber if you wish. I demand nothing more than what you have already given me.'

Orla sat on the edge of the bed and thought for a moment. He waited patiently, until she raised her head and said, 'I would like a child…for my farm and for myself.'

'With me?' he asked and there was no expectation in his question.

Her chest felt tight, as she contemplated her answer. She could ask him to leave her bed and go back to living as she always had, with that intimate aspect of life closed to her forever, or she could take a risk and learn the truth.

'Yes,' she said.

The firelight caught his blue eyes, so that they shone as brilliant as a summer sky. His large hand patted the empty space beside him. 'Come back to bed then, sweetheart.'

Willingly, she crawled back over him to the vacant side of the bed. It wasn't until she awkwardly tried to get back under the covers that she realised something. 'You could have just moved aside for me!' she grumbled.

'I like watching you crawl.'

Orla gave an indignant gasp. 'What a strange thing to say!' she snapped, as she tugged the covers primly over her body.

A rich chuckle filled the bed box. 'I like how the firelight shows off your curves…through the fabric of your shift… It is very thin.' He turned towards her, and pulled the blanket out of her numb fingers, tossing it down to the foot of the bed.

Twisting his body, he arched over her, covering her in his shadow. Sultry sapphires filled with heat washed over her and he fingered the ties of her shift lightly, as if he were a giant cat toying with her.

Her skin began to tingle with awareness, although whether it was fear or excitement, she couldn't be certain.

Reaching up with his hand, he swept aside some of the locks of red hair that covered her face. 'I presume you are innocent… Do you know what will happen?'

'I run a farm,' she said, a little bad-temperedly.

'I see,' he said, a languid smile stretching across his face. She could tell he found her answer amusing, but there was something knowing in his smile that made her heart flutter.

'I have heard it can be…joyous…with the right person.' As she spoke, his finger traced down her cheek to her neck and she struggled to catch her thoughts.

'I think you will enjoy it with me,' he said and for some reason she did not doubt him. She had known this man less than a day, yet she trusted everything he said.

His fingers trailed further down, skimming the line of her neck and her exposed collarbone, down the side of her breast, and then curving around the dip of her waist.

Her heart felt as if it were about to leap out of her chest and she sucked in a deep breath, hoping to calm it, fully aware that his palm now rested against her waist and was branding her skin with his presence.

'I hope so,' she whispered, reaching up to hold the top of his arm. His strength felt wonderful beneath her fingertips.

'Do you mind that I will not always be by your side?' he asked, leaning forward and brushing his lips against her mouth, in a way that made her question if she would mind anything that he did.

'I…' Her chest felt painfully tight, knowing that her next answer would decide her fate. 'I think I would prefer it.'

'I should be offended by that, but I am not.' He laughed, the sound rich and sweet like warmed mead. 'You love your home and your independence. I will not take it from you.'

She fought against her growing desire, wanting

things to be clear between them before they went any further. 'I am glad you understand. But…if there is a child—'

'They shall inherit your land. In Norway, my brothers are my heirs.'

She smiled. 'Then, yes, you are the right man for me.'

His gaze trailed from her eyes to her mouth and then to her collar. Now that the knot was open, he began to loosen the gathered ties of her neckline. He began to kiss her collarbone, butterfly touches that set her pulse racing. She wasn't sure what would happen, she only knew that she didn't want it to stop.

His hand moved down to her thigh, where he gathered up the lower fabric in his fist and then slowly dragged it up to her hip, his knuckles sliding against her bare skin.

Heat raced through her body and she could barely breathe because of the low ache between her legs. His chest was smooth and golden, and she moved her hands up his chest and shoulders to cup the back of his neck.

'Will you kiss me first? Like before…'

His mouth broadened into a wide smile. 'Did you like it when I kissed you?'

She nodded, her voice the barest of whispers. 'Yes… very much.'

He didn't reply. He leaned in to kiss her, pressing his hips against hers, the hard length of him rubbing against her until she let out a soft moan. Opening her mouth for him, she urged him silently to deepen the kiss. Enjoying the feel of him grinding against her. He moved with more urgency when he realised she was more than willing.

'Take it off,' he commanded, his eyes never leaving hers as he moved back a little to take off his braies. Quickly she pulled the shift over her head and set it aside, wishing she had not tied back the curtain after all, because she felt shy under his piercing gaze.

Covering herself as best she could with her arms, she lay back.

'There is no need to hide from me.' Lifting her wrists one at a time, he kissed her pulse points before draping her arms around his shoulders. 'You are so beautiful,' he said and she was sure she turned as bright as a berry with her blush.

He grinned at her reaction and she felt a momentary apprehension. 'Skalla was right… I have never shown interest in anyone before. They say I am cold in that regard. So, if I do not behave as other women—'

Hakon shook his head. 'I do not care what Skalla has said. That man is a spiteful idiot. You are capable of so much…joy… Let me prove it to you.'

His hand found its way between her thighs, and his eyes closed with a groan as he touched the wetness between them. 'You are almost ready for me,' he whispered, brushing his forehead against hers. Pressing a finger against the top of her entrance, he began to rub her in a steady rhythm.

A carnal moan erupted from her throat. Delighted by her reaction, Hakon chuckled against her mouth, the rich sound vibrating through her chest. 'See, you burn as brightly for me as I burn for you,' he whispered, his mouth brushing against her open lips, as if he wished to taste the moans of her desire.

Capturing her mouth in a breath-stealing kiss, he smothered her increasing moans of pleasure as his fingers drove her closer and closer to a climactic joy she had only ever experienced alone.

Instinctively, she opened her legs wider to aid him in his touch. Pressing kisses against her neck, he murmured roughly, 'You *are* passionate, my sweetling. You are perfect for me.'

His lips trailed down one breast. When his tongue swept lightly over her nipple, it was as if he had cracked a whip. Her back arched and her nails dug into his shoulders with a cry of pleasure, as her body shattered with release.

Hot damp heat pooled between her legs and he nudged her thighs a little wider, moving his large body so that he could kneel between them. His erection was thick and long, and her nervousness quickly returned at the sight of it.

'I will be gentle,' he promised her, pressing reassuring kisses against her lips and, as before, she believed him.

Her worries were quickly forgotten as she allowed the kiss to soothe away her fears with tender touches. Bracing one arm beside her head, he gathered one of her legs up, curving their bodies together like a bow as he slowly entered her. There was a sharp stretching and she gasped, but her discomfort was quickly eased as his length pushed forward, filling her with his heat and strength.

He groaned, his eyes closing as he savoured the feel of her. Slowly he withdrew from her body and then, with his head lowered, he sucked in a deep breath and rocked forward again, filling her more fully than before.

She cried out, but not from pain. The press of his pelvis against her core had reignited the pleasure from before and she tightened around him, like a fist clenching. Hakon whispered a curse, gritting his teeth as if he were in pain. He remained still for a moment, then rocked his hips forward and back with a sigh of pleasure.

Gripping his neck tightly, she pulled him down to press her mouth against his, desperate to satisfy his body, as he had hers. His tongue tasted her mouth and she moaned as he moved within her. Each time their bodies met he pressed his hips hard against hers and she felt another climax building between them.

He moved slowly in and out of her, until her need became too much and she began to match him with grinding thrusts of her own, her palms pressing against his buttocks demanding more. Their panting grew more urgent and heated, until Orla couldn't take it any more, waves of pleasure washing through her, drawing from her wild cries of ecstasy.

Holding her close, he thrust into her repeatedly, the leash on his control broken now that she had climaxed for a second time.

The bed box began to bang against the wall, and she tried her best not to giggle, her body limp and as light as a feather. Hakon exhaled with a sharp hiss, his head dipping to her neck as his release poured out of him, and his damp body slumped on top of hers.

She did not mind the weight of him pressed against her. Wrapping her arms around his shoulders, she trailed her fingers over his braid tenderly. It did not matter that their time together would be short. She had no more doubts and was glad she had taken this final step with him.

When he rolled to the side, he gathered her with him, as if he were unwilling to let her go. They slept entwined in each other's limbs and Orla knew she had made the right decision.

She would be grateful forever that he had come to her shores and agreed to marry her. She would rather have a moment of fleeting bliss than a lifetime of regret.

Chapter Nine

Hakon grunted as his scythe cut through the grass. He lifted the blade to the autumn light and sighed. 'I need to sharpen it again,' he said.

'No problem, there is so much still to collect anyway. You are cutting faster than we can pick up!' replied Wynflaed, out of breath, her face flushed.

Hakon stretched his back and examined the sky. It had been hot and humid for days, but the dark clouds rolling in from the east suggested the fine weather was about to break. 'We will need to have it all gathered in by tonight.'

People smiled and nodded in agreement as he passed them. The final days of summer were gone and autumn was a busy time of preparation. Everyone was working hard to cut the meadow, gather the grass and transport it to the barns. There it would be dried and turned repeatedly until it was fit for the animals.

He made his way to his supplies and noticed Orla walking back with the horse from the barn.

'I bought some refreshments, for when we are done.'

She removed a basket of oat cakes, a half-barrel of mead and a tall stack of cups from the saddle packs, and placed them on the ground. Then she began to help Gunnar load the waiting piles of hay into the horse's now-empty saddle packs.

Hakon rubbed a whetstone down the blade of his scythe, taking his time so that he could enjoy the sight of Orla bending over as she worked. She glanced over her shoulder at him and smiled. 'You *will* be done soon, will you not?'

He gave a sheepish shrug. 'Of course. There is not much left to do.'

She frowned at his words and straightened up to survey the field. 'Yes… Unfortunately.'

Knowing that she was worried about the shortage of hay, he walked to her side and wrapped one arm around her shoulders, giving her a light squeeze. 'I will fix it.'

Her expression brightened and she nodded. 'I know you will.' Lightly she shrugged off his arm and nudged him back towards the uncut side of the meadow. 'Back to work!' she ordered and he obeyed.

After Skalla's unexpected visit, he had not darkened their door again. Hakon knew Orla was hopeful it meant an end to their conflict. But he was not so certain—he imagined Skalla was merely licking his wounds.

So, Hakon's plan was to strengthen Orla's already good relationships with her neighbours, so that when the time came to demand part of Skalla's harvest in compensation, they would have other landholders' support.

Firstly, he had visited all of Orla's neighbours, trying to learn as much as possible about their connections and allegiances, while also appearing friendly and open himself. He had gone into each meeting thinking, *What would Egill do?* His younger brother was a natural-born diplomat.

It had worked. Even Snorri had welcomed him in the end, proudly showing off his bear to him and drinking plenty of ale deep into the night. Snorri was a loose-tongued drunk and had confessed that many did not support Skalla as much as they claimed. People believed Njal to be a brute and were even tiring of Skalla's high-handed ways.

Hakon was determined to play on each of their fears...although subtly. Any overt attack would be viewed with mistrust as he was still considered a stranger. So, in turn he reminded them regularly of Orla and her father's connection to the island and how well respected they were. So far, it appeared to be working.

He made short work of the remaining meadow and soon they only had one bale remaining to load into the barn. Everyone gathered in a circle on the newly shorn field and passed around oat cakes and mead to each other, taking a well-deserved rest in the fading heat of the day.

He tapped his cup against Orla's, as he sat down beside her. 'Skol!'

'Skol!' she replied and took a deep sip before adding, 'Thank you. You are the reason we managed to clear this field so quickly. You really are worth the price I paid for you.'

He laughed at her teasing. 'I am glad to hear it. Do you have much iron? I plan to use your smithy for the next few days.' He nodded towards the scythe lying a few feet away. 'You could do with some new tools... and some weapons. I might even train your men a little... They should know how to use them...just in case.'

Her pleasant expression dropped and he immediately regretted worrying her. 'I have some bog iron... But not much.'

Forcing a carefree smile, he nodded. 'Good, it would only be as a precaution.'

Orla's cheerfulness quickly returned. 'Yes, do whatever you wish. I cannot believe how much you have done already. If you are not seeing to the land or neighbours, you are repairing the buildings, or milking the cows... How are you never exhausted?'

'I have you and the hot pool to ease my aches each night.'

A rosy blush stained her cheeks and she turned away to sip her mead.

Hakon grinned at her prim response. She was a passionate woman by nature and he enjoyed teasing her. Although he would probably suffer for it later—she was equally playful in the bedchamber.

The workers began talking among themselves, laughing and teasing one another with ease. After being a jarl for so long, he had found the lack of hierarchy strange at first. He was not used to talking with people other than his brothers, especially not labourers, but he realised that was his own fault. He had maintained a prideful distance from his people, because it was what his parents had always done.

They believed in social order above all things. It was why he had been betrothed as a young man to a babe still in the womb, ridiculously waiting most of his youth for a girl to grow into a woman—sadly, she did not even make it to her tenth year. After her death, he had quickly formed a new alliance with his dead bride's cousin, hoping to still fulfil his late parents' wishes, only for that to crumble, too.

Looking back, he now saw how ridiculous such matches were. When he returned home, he would not seek another to stand by his side. No one could compare to his current wife.

Orla...

Warm, kind, honest Orla.

Every day he woke to find her up and dressed before him, ready to face the new day with a cheerful smile and a long list of tasks. Every night they talked over hearty meals, then made passionate love, until he fell asleep to the sound of her even breath.

'Your wounds have healed well,' Orla said, reaching out and gently tracing the scars on his wrist.

Grateful for any excuse, he took her hand in his. 'They have. Even the scars will fade in time.'

The marks on his wrists were the last to remain. The welts and bruises from his captivity were long gone, as if they had never happened.

'Are you still determined to seek vengeance?' she asked quietly, her eyes focused on their entwined hands, as if she found the sight fascinating. But there was tension in her jaw and he realised the significance of her question.

'My rage towards Ingvar has begun to cool. My need for vengeance feels like a far-away land…one I am no longer certain I wish to visit.'

What would he gain by killing Ingvar?

Revenge, of course, but what else? Somehow, it all seemed so pointless. A constant exchange of blows without purpose. He didn't even know the cause of the blood feud between them…no doubt some petty grievance from long ago.

If he won against Ingvar, he only opened himself to greater responsibilities and duties for King Harald.

Was that what he wanted?

He wasn't sure any more.

'You could stay a little longer… I would not mind.' She looked up at him then, her green eyes piercing his heart with hope.

With a deep breath of resignation, he said, 'Thank you. If it were not for my brothers… But I need to know what has happened to them.'

She nodded, her eyes dropping to shield her thoughts from view.

His brothers were the only tether still holding him to his old life and even that was beginning to ease a little. Maybe it was the good food, the comfortable bed or the fiery woman by his side, but he was beginning to feel more optimistic about his brothers' fate.

'I hope they are well,' Orla said and he knew she meant it.

'I think they are. I think I would feel it if they were

not… They were badly wounded, but they are the strongest, most resilient men I know.'

'I always wanted a sibling… Tell me about them—are they like you?'

'Well… Grimr is only younger than me by two years. He is strong and vicious, but also deeply loyal. I am certain he would have found a way to escape and evade Ingvar's men. While Egill, our youngest brother, has always had a serpent tongue. He could charm anyone with his words, or cut them down just as easily with a blade. Even if Ingvar tells lies about what happened, Egill will make the King see the truth of it, or will at least twist it in our favour.'

'They sound like good brothers. I am sure they survived.' She squeezed his hand, offering both comfort and reassurance.

He nodded. 'I agree. Every day, I am more convinced that they escaped and lived. They will have gathered an army and sought revenge. If Ingvar survived long enough, they might discover what has happened to me and they will come for me.'

Her expression brightened. 'Then you should stay longer… You would not want to miss them if they did come for you.'

He smiled, lifting her hand to his mouth and pressing a kiss against it. Strangely, he was happy to wait for them. No longer was he consumed with plans to leave Iceland as soon as he was able. 'Yes, perhaps I should… A year, maybe? And then I will go back to see what became of them.'

'That sounds…fair,' she said, turning her face towards the sun and closing her eyes, letting the light bathe her in golden beauty.

After all, there were only two possibilities that awaited him: either his brothers would kill Ingvar and rule his jarldom without him, or they were dead and he had nothing waiting for him except revenge.

If his brothers ruled his land, why would he need to rush back? They were his heirs, anyway, and could easily fulfil his fealty to the King.

Grimr was ambitious and his unwavering loyalty to him as jarl had cost him a future of his own. Maybe he would believe Hakon had died and they would not come for him? If that were the case, he wasn't sure if he wanted to leave Orla...ever.

Chapter Ten

The next day the fine weather broke and rain poured from the sky as if the gods were trying to drown them.

'So, what do you think?' Hakon asked Gunnar as they stomped in from the autumn storm. Thor was beating his hammer loudly, and flashes of lightning split the pewter sky. The weather had been fine that morning, but had changed dramatically over the afternoon.

Another couple of sheep had gone missing. He had gone with Gunnar to check the perimeter and ensure there were no breaks in the fences, or accidental deaths. There was no sign of either. The sheep had not wandered away, they had been stolen—which only confirmed what they had originally suspected.

There had been some muddy tracks around one section of the fence. But there was no clear indication of where they led to, only that they bordered Snorri's land.

'Either Snorri is the thief or someone wants us to think Snorri is the thief,' replied Gunnar, taking off his cloak and shaking off the water before hanging it on a peg. Hakon did the same and they made their way to the fire, warming away the chill from their hands.

'I imagine Snorri would happily steal a sheep or two if he could get away with it.'

Gunnar snorted. 'Of course, he is an opportunist and would happily have any extra meat for his bear. But I cannot imagine him going out of his way to steal. More likely he would grab animals that wandered into his fields by mistake and not go out of his way to pick them off one by one, as he would risk being caught.'

Hakon nodded thoughtfully, rubbing hands together and letting the heat seep back into his bones. 'I agree. Move the sheep to the field nearest the hall. Regardless of who has been taking them, they seem to prefer trespassing into our lands from there. If we take away the opportunity, we reduce the risk of more thefts.'

'True. We may need to slaughter half of the sheep, anyway, to get us through the winter and keep the cattle fed. But then we will not have as many lambs in the spring and that will affect our wool production and supplies for many years to come.'

Hakon patted the older man's arm to console him. 'I still plan to demand hay from Skalla. But if we are forced to deplete our stock, then I will go to Norway in the spring and return by the autumn with plenty of silver, sheep and supplies to make up for it. Let us focus on surviving this winter first and not worry about what is to come.'

'You would go all the way to Norway and return within one season?' asked Gunnar with a raised brow. 'I did not think that was part of the deal.'

So much was no longer part of the deal.

'Orla is my wife,' he answered firmly. 'And I will always provide for and support her. When I swear an oath, it is never broken.'

What of your vow to your brothers? You also made a vow to seek revenge!

Gunnar gave him a wide, gummy smile. 'She picked well then—but Orla was always a wise buyer.'

Had she picked well?

If he returned to Norway, could he really return to Iceland so easily? Already he felt as if he were making false promises, by saying he would stay for a year. What if his brothers *were* dead? Could he leave their vengeance to fate, possibly allow Ingvar to succeed in his absence?

Doubts filled his mind and he wanted to see Orla more than anything—she always eased his mind. He glanced around the weaving looms and kitchen to be sure he hadn't missed her the first time he walked in, but she was nowhere to be seen.

'Where is Mistress Orla?' he asked Mildritha, as she passed by them with a bucket of herbs and vegetables for the evening meal.

'In her rooms, I think,' she said with a frown, 'although I have not seen her for some time.'

A loud crack of thunder rumbled overhead and Gunnar gestured to the ceiling with a leathery finger. 'She will be hiding from the storm. Thankfully, we do not get many this far south.'

Confused by Gunnar's words, he decided to seek Orla out and learn the truth.

Was she afraid of storms?

He couldn't imagine brave, fierce Orla was afraid of anything. She was always so hopeful, so cheerful and courageous in the face of any challenge.

She had accepted him into her bed without hesitation, knowing that she had committed herself to a life with an absent husband and father. Bringing up any child they might have alone.

She deserved better.

'Orla?' he called softly as he entered her chamber. The fire was all but a few embers, all shutters closed to keep out the wind and rain. He put a log on the brazier and stirred up the ash so that it would catch.

Light bloomed, but it was still gloomy and dark within the chamber. The bed's heavy curtains were down, but when another loud boom cracked overhead, he thought he heard a whimper coming from inside the bed box.

Kicking off his boots, he pulled aside the fabric. Orla lay beneath the covers, one of the feather pillows pressed over her head.

'Orla, are you well?'

'Yes, I am fine, thank you,' mumbled a voice from beneath, but it was obvious by the trembling of her body that she was lying.

He pulled up the corner of the blanket and slipped beneath to join her.

The pillow raised a little and he could just make out the shape of her features in the darkness. 'Honestly, I am fine… I just don't like—' Another bang of Thor's hammer filled the air and she yelped. Throwing aside the pillow, she burrowed against him, pressing her ear to his chest and covering the other with her hand.

Instinctively, he pulled her closer, wrapping an arm around her head so that she wouldn't have to hold her ear. Another drop of the hammer followed shortly after and she whimpered, wrapping her arm around his side and fisting the cloth of his tunic in her hand.

'This is so stupid!' she snapped angrily at herself, even as she snuggled closer to him.

'No, it is not.' He pulled her closer, liking that she found comfort in his arms. He basked in the feel of her lush body pressed up against his. 'It will pass soon,' he reassured her, lowering his chin a little so he could breathe in the scent of her hair. Lamb's wool, hay and heather mixed with the warm musk of her body, and he sighed with pleasure.

Another bang filled the air and she clutched him even tighter with a pitiful groan. Wickedly, his body tightened in response and he had to focus on the wall of the bed box to stop from embarrassing himself like a green youth.

'Have you always been frightened of storms?' he asked, hoping the distraction would ease his discomfort.

She nodded, her hair brushing beneath his chin. 'Since I was a child. I was captured in a storm…that probably has a lot to do with it. I was young and it is all that I remember about the raid. The thunder and lightning, the smoke…the screams.'

His heart ached for the terrified little girl she must

have been and impulsively he kissed the top of her head. 'You are safe with me.'

'I know.' She sighed. 'It is in the past… I hate that I am being such a coward right now. Please tell me something frightens you, too… Battle, perhaps?'

He could tell she was seeking a distraction and not accusing him of dishonour, so he didn't take offence at her question and thought about it carefully for a moment before answering. 'Battle does not scare me. When I fight, a strange calmness takes a hold over me. I focus only on the next swing of my sword or the raise of my shield. It is a beautiful dance in my mind and my body knows the steps instinctively after so many years of practice… And, I believe there is no need to be afraid. The day of our death has already been chosen by the Norns and I accept the will of the gods in that regard. I cannot avoid my fate, only live and fight well until my time comes.'

She chuckled lightly. 'You must think me as pitiful as a babe in comparison…to be afraid of a little bad weather.'

'I think you are very brave to have suffered so much as a child.'

'Oddr, my father, was very kind and patient. He had lost his wife that winter and had no children of his own. He once said that seeing me arrive into port had felt like a gift from the gods. His wife had always wanted a daughter and it felt as if she were placing me in his arms as her final wish. I was lucky to have him…' She paused. Then, as if she had seen the secret behind his words, she asked, 'Have you truly never been scared?'

'I have. The day I woke up in chains, I was terrified. Not because I had lost my freedom, but because…' He struggled to find the words and she raised her head from his chest.

'Because?' she urged him, with a gentle kindness he found deeply comforting.

'I was afraid I had lost them…my brothers.'

'That is understandable.'

'No, it is not,' he said with a dry chuckle. 'My brothers regularly fight by my side. I have even sent them into battle knowing they may die. It never troubled me before, because I knew they would fight with honour and skill, trusting that if it was their fate to die then it was the will of the gods, and that I would fall soon after. But…when Ingvar turned on us, I felt helpless… I could not understand why the gods would punish me, and support Ingvar instead.

'We were unarmed and outnumbered. It wasn't a test of our skills or courage, but a desperate scramble for survival. Then everything went black and, when I awoke, I did not know if they were dead or alive. I am still uncertain, although I hope they are. But those first few moments of uncertainty were…*terrible*. I could not bear to think of them being gone and leaving me behind. I had not realised, until then, how afraid I was to lose them.'

He could not see her expression, but there was a soft sadness in her tone as she answered, 'But…losing people is the only certainty in life and when I hear thunder, I am reminded of that awful truth.'

His arms tightened around her. 'It is not *so* awful… We are only afraid to lose them because we love them.'

'Maybe it is better not to love?' she said lightly and his heart tightened.

Was that why she had never married? Because she was afraid to lose more people?

'No,' he answered firmly, before explaining, 'because if Oddr had never loved his wife, he never would have freed a little slave girl and called her his daughter.'

'True,' she replied and he realised that she was no longer trembling and the storm's rage had died down to a soft murmur. Despite this, she still clung to him as she had before.

Her hand wrapped around his middle and his heart began to ache.

They understood each other.

Orla did not want to lose him and he could not abandon his brothers. Their time was short, but they would savour what they could.

Chapter Eleven

'Snorri's bear is loose!' cried Mildritha, bursting into the hall breathless, her face sickly pale and sweat beading her brow. Orla had been scared before Mildritha had even opened her mouth.

Damn the storm! Bad things always followed.

'Is anyone hurt?' asked Hakon, rising from his seat.

Mildritha swallowed nervously, her eyes dipping to the floor as she shook her head. 'No, but it is by the eastern meadows near the cattle. Please hurry!' There were tears in her eyes and he wondered if she had been frightened by the sight of it.

'Don't worry, Mildritha,' he reassured her with a pat to her arm. 'I have hunted bears before. They are strong, but stupid, and I always bring everyone home.'

'I will get you a bow and a spear,' Orla said, jumping to her feet and heading to one of the chests. Quickly she removed the hunting weapons and handed them to him.

'I may need more than that,' Hakon said, leaving the room and returning quickly with her father's axe and shield, a wide smile on his face that looked far too cheerful.

'You could seem a little less pleased about it!' she snapped. 'That's more of our precious livestock potentially lost.'

He shrugged. 'I will demand recompense.'

'Snorri will not like it. He loves that bear.'

'Then he should not have allowed the bear to escape.'

That eased some of her concern, but not by much. 'Should we all come with you? It may be easier with more people.'

'No, it would cause only chaos. None of you is a trained fighter. Besides, I have killed bears before... I will be fine.' Orla frowned and opened her mouth to argue, but he pressed a kiss to her lips and then grinned. 'There is no need to worry. I will return shortly.'

He walked away from her with a swagger in his step, as if he were off to a feast and not facing a wild beast. When Orla turned back to the hall, she noticed Mildritha crying in the corner and went to comfort her.

Hakon turned to Gunnar at the hall's entrance and spoke quietly to him. 'Gather the people and lock yourselves in the hall. Tell Orla it is just a precaution. But do not open for anyone but me.'

Gunnar frowned, but nodded, and began to call to the women to come inside.

Tyr and Valdar were the only young men of fighting age in the household and they brought over horses. Mounting them quickly, they left the farm and headed towards the eastern meadows.

Valdar turned to him with a worried expression. 'I have never hunted a bear before. What is the best way?'

'With spears and arrows…but I doubt there is a bear waiting for us.'

'What do you mean?' asked Tyr, obviously confused.

'Have you seen Wynflaed this morning?'

The two men looked at each other and shook their heads.

'Neither have I,' said Hakon, 'and I have only seen Mildritha this frightened once before—when she and her sister were captured. It is a trap and I suspect they have Wynflaed. Hopefully they are planning on just killing me, but, just in case, I have told Gunnar to gather the women and lock them in the hall.'

'Then…what should we do? We can't let them kill you or Wynflaed,' said Tyr.

Hakon smiled at their support, but shook his head. 'We will circle around to the back of the eastern meadow. There is a coppice of trees there. I am sure that is where they are hiding…but we shall surprise them instead. I know you are not experienced in battle, but try your best and let me lead the charge.'

Valdar gave a grim nod. 'We have learned a lot from your weapons training, we will not let you down.'

Tyr nodded in agreement and Hakon was glad he had taken the time to practise with them.

His suspicions about an ambush were quickly confirmed. They had tied their horses up a field away and made the rest of the journey through the trees on foot.

The coppice was quiet. As they crept towards the

eastern meadow, they saw the carcass of a cow at the edge of the tree-line. The body had been slashed and gutted to appear as if Snorri's bear had attacked it.

Within the trees to the side lay the body of Snorri's bear. Hakon would guess its white fur, seen from a distance, would have been enough to lure someone into the trees. But the poor animal's throat was slit, the chain Snorri had used to lead it still attached. Hakon could see their plan as clearly as if Njal had laid it out like a map.

Snorri's bear would be blamed for Hakon and his men's deaths. Njal would claim he'd stumbled upon the bear feasting on their bones and immediately killed it. Such a tale would dispose of Hakon without staining either Skalla's or Njal's reputation.

In the undergrowth lay several armed men, watching and waiting for his arrival... Except they were all facing the wrong direction.

A flash of ochre skirt belonging to Wynflaed caught his eye. She was tied and gagged on the ground, but otherwise unhurt. He wondered what they would do with her after. He imagined they would release her, making sure both sisters swore never to tell the truth. After all, who would believe two newly freed slave girls over a powerful family? Only Orla, and they would not care about her opinion, would probably prefer it if she began to fear them.

Njal was among the men and they were so preoccupied searching the hillside for sight of Hakon that they did not notice him creeping towards them from behind. He gave the signal to Tyr and Valdar, then they attacked, his men sending arrows into the legs of the nearest men. Their screams alerted Njal and the others. As they turned, Hakon burst forward with a battle cry.

He had instructed Tyr and Valdar to hold back and use all their arrows before moving forward. They had surprise on their side and Hakon was confident enough with his skills that he knew he could take most of the men alone.

Wynflaed had the good sense to get to her feet and run. Even though her hands were tied, she managed well until she tried to pass Njal. He grabbed her by the hair, pulling her back. Hakon knocked two men down with his shield, but kept running. A man with a sword and shield attacked him and he battled with him, trying his best to manoeuvre enough to reach Wynflaed.

Njal was shouting at her, 'Your sister betrayed us— your blood is on her hands!' while pushing her backwards. She fell to the ground and he raised his sword above her, ready to slice her in two.

Hakon threw his axe and it struck Njal in the chest with a heavy thud. Njal flopped backwards, his sword still raised high, but his eyes already glassy with death. Without a weapon, Hakon used his shield to protect himself against the attack from the remaining man.

The skirmish was almost over. He just needed to kill this last man. The rest were screaming on the floor in agony—they were not seasoned warriors. 'Why don't you take the wounded back to Skalla?' he shouted to his opponent. Until he found himself a weapon he would be locked in this ridiculous fight forever. The man could not match his skills with a blade, but Hakon could not kill him without one.

The young man shook his head, beads of sweat on his brow. 'Skalla said to kill you or never return.'

'Hakon!' called one of his men, throwing him a sword. Hakon used it to hook and throw aside the man's axe.

The man stared in horror at the loss of his weapon and then raised his shield with a determined grit of his teeth.

'Do you have family?' asked Hakon, pausing a moment. 'I only ask because I wonder if you would consider joining me… I am short of men.'

The man's eyes widened, but he noticed a glimmer of hope reflected within. 'I have brothers…and a sister.'

Hakon nodded, looking the man firmly in the eye. 'Go. If you come to my hall before nightfall, I will accept all of you.'

The man nodded, then sprinted away.

'What if he goes to Skalla?' asked Tyr.

'Then I will have to kill him tonight instead of today,' replied Hakon.

'Tonight?'

Hakon nodded grimly. 'Yes, Skalla has no choice now—he has to attack us openly, or lose everything.'

Orla's heart was hammering in her chest as she strode with the other women towards the eastern meadow. Gunnar had tried to insist they stay inside, but she was still mistress of her hall and would not accept Hakon's orders, no matter how well intentioned.

Neither would any of the other women. When Mildritha had confessed the truth, they'd all grabbed whatever weapon they could find and charged out to join with Orla. Tyr's and Valdar's wives were the first to join her, with bows and arrows in hand.

They didn't have many weapons, even after Hakon's work in the smithy, so some carried pitchforks, axes or butcher knives instead, anything to help them in a fight.

It appeared their show of strength was unnecessary, because Hakon and his men came riding back across the fields before they had made it halfway there.

Relief and joy washed through her when she saw they were all unharmed, including Wynflaed, who dropped down from the horse and ran into her sister's waiting arms.

However, Hakon looked furious. 'Damn it, Gunnar! I told you to lock them in the hall!' he bellowed and Gunnar glared at his mistress accusingly.

'He was outnumbered. Besides, I am still mistress here. And as your *wife*, my word is final in your absence.'

'Not when it goes against my order!' he snapped back, handing his reins to Tyr and dismounting from his horse in one smooth motion.

When he strode towards her, she wondered if he would shout at her some more. But to her surprise he grabbed hold of her and crushed her to him in a fierce embrace. The spear fell from her hand and she hugged him back.

'I could not leave you to face them alone,' she whispered.

'I knew it was an ambush. There was no need for you to worry,' he murmured softly against her hair.

She sucked in a deep calming breath, allowing her mind and body to accept that he was safe and well… before whacking him hard in the arm. 'Tell me next time!' she yelled, then pulled him down again so that she could bury her face in his neck.

After a moment she turned back to her people, wiping tears from her eyes. 'Wynflaed, are you well?' she asked, reaching for her, and Wynflaed fell into her arms.

'I am so sorry, Mistress! Please do not punish Mildritha for lying.'

'Of course not!' snapped Orla, as if her fears were ridiculous, and Hakon couldn't help but smile.

But then he remembered the current threat looming over them. 'I killed Njal. I am sorry, I could not avoid it. But it means Skalla will seek vengeance against us. We should prepare for an immediate attack. We should tell our neighbours about what happened…they might rally to our side, if they learn the truth.'

Orla nodded. 'I have already sent the children out as messengers to the surrounding farms. But I do not know if they will side with Skalla or with us—he has blood oaths from many of them.'

Hakon hooked his arm around her shoulders and brushed a quick kiss against her lips. 'We shall see. Let us prepare as if no one will come and hope the gods favour us.'

Chapter Twelve

Hakon barked orders and people ran to obey. 'Tyr, take five people and pour water over the hall doors. The recent rain has soaked the turf so we should be safe against fire as long as the doors are wet. Do the same to the barns if you have time, but they are not our priority.

'Gunnar, gather as many weapons as you can and sharpen them. Valdar, put ladders against the beams inside and cut some holes. We will fire arrows from them later.

'Wynflaed, gather stones and wood, anything you can throw at the enemy, and pile it inside. Bring in anything we can use or that could be used against us to form a barricade at the entrances of the hall. Don't forget the tunnel at the back… Although, don't block it just yet, we may have to use it in a retreat—so have a cart ready to drag across it.'

'Someone is coming,' Orla said, shading her eyes from the low sun as she squinted at the men in the distance. 'It can't be Skalla yet, it will take him time to gather men and march over here from his lands.'

Hakon came to stand by her side. 'Ahh, it is probably the youth I spared…he said he had brothers and a sister. I offered them sanctuary if they joined with us.'

'I recognise him…he is a decent man. But there are a lot of people with him…more than his family.'

As the group of about fifteen men and one woman arrived, there was one face that truly surprised her. 'Snorri? Have you come to my aid, Neighbour? I always thought you disapproved of me.'

The sour-faced man's eyes were red with rage. 'Is it true? Has that bastard killed my Bjarni Bear to lure you into an ambush?'

Orla never thought she would feel sympathy for a man as bad-tempered as Snorri, but she did. The grief he felt for his bear was obvious. Even though she had always disapproved of him keeping the beast as a pet, she had to admit he *had* cared for it. 'Yes, I am so sorry, Bjarni did not deserve his fate.'

'Will you stand with us?' asked Hakon.

'I will.' Snorri gave a loud sniff of disdain. 'Skalla is getting too ambitious for my liking. If he takes over your land, he will control most of the southern region. And, I would prefer you as my neighbour,' he admitted, although he would not meet her eyes.

Orla smiled. 'I am glad you are here, Snorri. Thank you.'

Snorri shrugged in answer, then began to order his men to help with Hakon's orders.

* * *

He wasn't the only man to come that afternoon. A few other more distant farmers arrived before nightfall and Orla welcomed them with food and gratitude.

'Who knew I had so many friends?' she murmured to herself, as she filled a quiver with arrows.

'Why would you ever doubt it?' asked Gunnar, with a gummy smile that warmed her heart. Gunnar was helping Hakon move a bench to the barricade as he added, 'It is good that you met with them, Hakon. I think it reassured them.'

Surprised, she turned to her husband. 'You met with them?'

Hakon nodded. 'I greeted each one as I learned about your land. Do you mind? I was only introducing myself as your husband.'

'Mind?' She smiled. 'Honestly, I am grateful. You have helped in so many ways…'

Hakon's expression took on a grim countenance. 'I have also made it worse for you.'

She shook her head. 'No, this was always going to happen and I would much rather have you and my friends by my side—whatever happens.'

The sun was hanging low in the sky when Skalla arrived. Unlike his last visit, he was no longer alone. Orla's heart leapt into her throat when she saw he had nearly a hundred men with him: warriors, loyal farmers, labourers and thralls. Skalla had emptied out most of his land to meet with them.

She and the other women were positioned on a

newly built platform in the rafters where they could rain arrows down upon their attackers. The newly carved arrow opening felt rough beneath her fingers, but she didn't care, gripping it tightly even as splinters pierced her skin.

May the gods protect us…and my husband. Please save him most of all.

Hakon and the rest of the fighting men waited in a long line outside the hall doors, with shields and blades at the ready. They would fight them off for as long as they could, then retreat down the side of the hall to the hot springs entrance, while Orla and her people covered their escape from above. After that, they would try to keep them out of the hall for as long as possible. They were outnumbered, but breaching the hall would cost Skalla many of his men.

'Get ready with your arrows!' said Orla, as she threaded her bow and aimed it.

'You should have taken my offer the first time, Hakon!' roared Skalla, as he led his pack of men into their farm. 'You killed my son and now you will die!'

'Your son deserved his death. At least you have the decency to attack me openly, unlike your son!' Hakon retorted, banging his shield with her father's axe to punctuate his anger.

Skalla sneered. 'You are still outnumbered, fool!' He raised his sword, signalling his men to charge. They ran forward and her women's arrows dropped a couple of them. But they were not trained with the weapon and many missed their mark. It was enough to give their attackers pause and many stumbled or raised their shields before they reached the hall doors.

Hakon's shield wall remained intact as a wave of men crashed into them. They pounded on his shields, sharp blades trying to slip between the gaps to pierce their only line of defence.

It would be a difficult fight, but Hakon and the rest of the men were braced for the onslaught. With a rallying cry they hit back at their attackers with sword and axe as their wives, daughters and sisters struck at their enemy from above.

Orla started throwing stones from the windows. They had run out of arrows quickly, but the men kept on coming, no matter how many Hakon and his men cut down. They slammed into their shield wall with disturbing force, the cracking of shields sounding like thunder in her ears. But she refused to run and hide. They were managing the impossible and keeping Skalla from their door.

The sun was almost gone and a flickering light in the distance grabbed her attention. A line of torches was heading towards them from the south.

Surely not reinforcements?

They had to be. Skalla had allegiances far and wide. But Orla had called on all her friends…there was no one left.

Fear engulfed her heart, threatening to strip her of all hope.

'Hakon!' she screamed, trying to draw his attention, but her voice did not reach him through the chaos of battle below. 'They need to retreat!' she cried and the women stared at her in confusion—they had not seen the line of torches yet.

She ran to the platform edge and flew down the ladder, missing several steps in her haste and practically falling down most of it.

'Be careful, Mistress!' shouted Mildritha from above.

Running to the barricaded door, she began to yank away furniture, the pieces cracking and falling at her feet.

'Let me help you!' said Wynflaed, and Orla hadn't even noticed that the women had followed her. With their help she managed to slip through the tightly packed blockade and squeezed through the narrow opening.

The men and their shield wall were tightly packed against the door, so she barely got her body out before she was shouting in her husband's ear. 'Hakon! Retreat! There are more men coming!' she shouted, having to twist her body to the side as a sharp spear stabbed through a gap between Hakon's and Gunnar's shields.

Hakon glanced back at her, and then yelled, 'Gunnar, get her back!'

Gunnar tried to step back, but the men in front sensed a breach and hammered even harder against them.

'Stay, Gunnar! I am going—you must retreat, Hakon! You must! Do it now before it is too late!' She slipped back through the doorway and the women quickly pushed back the blockade.

'Get back up! We need to protect their retreat!' she ordered and the women flew back towards the ladders. 'We need more things to throw! Grab whatever you can! Stones, logs, pots…anything!'

They scurried around the hall like rats on a sinking ship. Wynflaed even smashed a chair into pieces, then handed the wood to women as they climbed back up the ladders.

In a horrifyingly short time, the sound of more men joining the fray rolled in like a blizzard. Screams filled the air and Orla's face went numb with fear. She rushed to her arrow hole and peered out.

She gasped at the sight below her and some of the women hugged one another, tears flowing like rain. The men who had joined the fight were not adding to those attacking the hall. Instead, they were fighting Skalla and his men from behind, cutting them down like wheat.

'They aren't Skalla's reinforcements,' Wynflaed gasped. Mildritha peeked over her shoulder and then cheered, hugging her sister from behind, as they bounced with joy.

'But…who are they? Everyone I know that is loyal has already come!' asked Orla, straining to see more clearly.

'Does it matter? We are saved!' Mildritha laughed.

The torches of their saviours had been cast aside, slowly dying in the muddy earth. The daylight was also fading rapidly as the battle slowed.

'But…how will we ever repay them?' whispered Orla, afraid of what was to come.

Hakon's heart soared when he realised his brothers had come to join the fight. He had been preparing himself for the final retreat. He had given instructions to

Gunnar that, if things were to turn sour, then he was to take the women and escape to Snorri's hall.

He hoped Skalla's bloodlust would be satisfied with Hakon's death. However, Orla's earlier actions had worried him—she was not biddable and he loved that about her. But she had risked her own safety to warn him and he could not allow her to do such a thing.

It was the first time he had been truly afraid in battle, where panic and terror had overcome his usual calm and practised resolve. He no longer wished to leave the future in the hands of the gods. He wanted to beg and plead for mercy, to make deals and offer his life in exchange for hers.

Anything to keep her safe.

He had been afraid. Not for himself, but for Orla, and for what she might do...*for him*! What if she refused to leave without him? She would die, that much was certain—her uncle's pretence was over and he wanted her land. All respect for her father's wishes had died with Njal and he was the one to blame. He almost regretted saving Wynflaed, which felt a terrible thing to admit, but if he had not killed Njal then this blood feud might never have happened.

Orla had married him to keep her safe and for a moment he thought he had failed her. If he were to leave this world, then he wanted the only thing he valued to remain. To save Orla, because she was precious to him.

Thankfully, it had not come to that. As was the way with life and war, the tide turned within a heartbeat, as more men arrived to help them. The shield wall broke, but not through defeat—it surged forward and out to meet their saviours.

He recognised every face: they were his friends, his warriors, his brothers.

'Hakon! Who are our new friends?' laughed Egill as he hacked his way to Hakon's left side, men flying to the sides of him as he cut them down.

'My new family…although I do not think they like me,' he replied cheerfully, banging his shield against his brother's in greeting.

'We heard you got married,' Grimr said, moving to his right side and turning his shield to protect Hakon's flank. 'I hope she was worth it!' There was a dark expression to his last words that sounded almost bitter, but as Hakon was busy fighting he didn't question it.

Skalla shouted to his own men, 'Shield wall, you stupid rats! Shield wall!'

But only half of the men were sworn warriors to Skalla—the rest were labourers and farmers, their loyalty fragile and balanced like trading scales. Hakon had no heart to kill men that were only here out of service.

'Put your weapons down!' he shouted. 'Pledge your loyalty to my house and I will forgive you!' Hakon stepped forward to face Skalla's shield wall.

Hesitantly, the men's gazes shifted between him and Skalla, weighing up their options.

'He has no place here! He is not one of us!' Skalla stepped forward, his face flushed with anger and humiliation.

'I will not die so that you can double your power, Skalla!' shouted one of the men, throwing down his weapon. 'Njal was a deceitful fool. He *did* deserve his death and you know it! Odin's teeth, he attacked your *niece*!'

'Niece? She is a slave girl, who is owed nothing! She has no right to my brother's land,' snarled Skalla dismissively.

'She is a freed woman and your brother's heir. You agreed to her inheritance in front of all the elders. It is against the law to defy his wishes!' growled a farmer, as he tossed his axe to the ground.

'Silence!' screamed Skalla. 'Or I shall strip you of your farmstead!'

This had the opposite effect to the one Skalla had intended. The crowd began to mutter with revulsion and disapproval.

'I never wanted to swear fealty to you in the first place!' snapped one man, throwing down his sword. 'Njal threatened to hurt my daughter if I refused to pledge my allegiance. I am glad he is dead!'

'You promised me a cow!' came another voice from the crowd.

'Liar!' shouted Skalla, although there was a wildness to his eyes as he glanced around at the men turning from him.

'You are the liar, Skalla!' sneered another man. 'Where is the land you promised me? You have so much already and *still* you want more!'

The farmer from before nodded and he pointed an accusing finger at Skalla. 'Now we see the heart of it. Your greed rules you. You care nothing for your brother's wishes and have done nothing but steal sheep and torment Mistress Orla for weeks. You did not even help her bury him, yet you claim his property as if it were your own? What is to stop you from taking ours next!'

Skalla's eyes widened as he realised how quickly he was losing his support. Some of his men had already started walking away, taking some of the wounded with them. Others were not done with him and turned on him with growing menace in their eyes.

Desperate to regain his control, he swivelled towards Hakon and pointed accusingly. 'He is to blame! This stranger! This self-named jarl! He is—' Skalla's eyes widened suddenly as his voice and air were taken from him.

He fell to the ground, a knife in his back, and Snorri stepped out from behind him. Hakon had not even noticed the man weaving into the opposition's ranks.

Snorri's voice was as cold as ice. 'For Bjarni!' he said.

Banging from within the hall was quickly followed by Orla swinging open the doors and rushing to his side. More women poured out, carrying torches and embracing their loved ones with tearful kisses.

'You are safe!' she gasped, hugging him tightly before forcing herself to take a dignified step back.

Snorri's eyes swept over the crowd, before focusing on Hakon. 'Skalla's land should be divided between those he has harmed. Mistress Orla will receive the majority as she is his only living kin. But I, and those who stood beside you today, should also receive our fair share... Do you agree?'

Hakon turned to his wife. 'Orla, it was your uncle who wronged you with his betrayal. What say you?'

Orla nodded. 'Snorri, I think it best that not one family hold too much power, and my land is already large. However, Skalla did take much from me and not only in livestock. I will require supplies and compensation to survive the winter. But I am sure we can come to an arrangement that suits all of us.

'However, first we must protect the families of the dead—they should not suffer for Skalla's deceit. So, come to me *after* we have buried my uncle with your suggestions, and my husband and I will discuss it with you further.'

Hakon smiled at the clever and compassionate way Orla had dealt with the issue—she truly was a formidable woman. She had given herself enough time to consider what she would need, as well as how best to manage the distribution so that no one could wield too much power over her ever again.

Snorri also seemed pleased with her answer and Hakon would probably advise Orla to agree to his terms—as long as they were reasonable. It seemed that the landowners here feared a man with too much power and he did not want to put Orla in a precarious position by insisting she take too much of it…

Especially if he wasn't going to stay.

His brothers had come so quickly…was Ingvar still alive? Had King Harald ordered his return? So much was still uncertain.

He glanced at his brothers. It was good to see them,

but it was a bittersweet kind of joy. Soon, everything would change…

Permanently, and he wasn't sure if he was ready.

The men began to disperse, carrying with them the dead and injured. Thankfully, there were not many and even fewer from their side.

Orla was pale in the moonlight and he cupped her face with his hands. 'Are you well?'

She nodded, but glanced nervously towards his brothers. 'We have guests… Are they your brothers?'

'You can tell?' he teased, knowing full well that they all bore a striking similarity to each other. They were all tall, broad, golden and blue-eyed. But that was where the similarity ended—their personalities were very different from one another.

'Yes,' she answered softly, her green eyes watching his brothers with curious trepidation.

Hakon swept an arm around her shoulders and pulled her close. 'I am not surprised. Our mother used to say we were poured into the same mould. She constantly muddled our names up as children—in the end she just called us *her boys*.'

He smiled at the memory; his mother had always been gentler and wiser than his father. She would have loved Orla… *He* loved Orla.

The realisation did not shock him, strangely. It had crept up on him like sleep, slowly possessing him from the inside out, and he found he did not mind that he had given her his heart. It felt…inevitable.

Not liking the fearful way she continued to stare at his brothers, he reached down and nudged her chin lightly with his knuckle. Her face tilted towards him, her moss-green eyes softened ever so slightly under his gaze, and he brushed a reassuring kiss against her lips. 'You are safe,' he murmured and she released her breath with a grateful sigh.

'As are you,' she said.

When he next looked up, his brothers were staring at them, Egill with open astonishment, while Grimr's head was tilted with cool curiosity. He supposed it was because he had never acted this way with a woman before.

'Hakon, will you not introduce us to our new sister?' asked Egill with a wide grin.

Orla stepped away from him, a blush high on her cheeks. She smiled warmly at Egill, although she glanced warily at Grimr. Most people found Grimr intimidating, so he was not surprised, although he wished for once that his brother would not look at *everyone* with suspicion.

'Orla, these are my brothers. My youngest brother, Egill, and my heir, Grimr.'

Grimr scowled at the word *heir*. Hakon knew it was because he hated the idea of succeeding him.

Orla gave a deep bow of appreciation. 'Thank you for coming to our aid. I will gather the women and prepare a feast to welcome you and your men.'

'They are your husband's men. Not mine,' Grimr replied curtly, and Orla gave him a nervous smile of agreement before hurrying inside.

Rolling his eyes, Egill jabbed his brother in the ribs. 'Can you at least try to be pleasant, for *once*?'

Grimr ignored him and turned to Hakon. 'Ingvar's

sister confessed to your enslavement, but I am sorry we did not come sooner. It is Sigrid's fault, she is like her brother, full of *tricks…*' He snarled the last word and Hakon pitied the woman, even if she had been the one to persuade Ingvar to sell him into slavery. He had hated her at first, but now he wondered if he should thank her.

'What became of her?' he asked, not liking the fire in his brother's eyes.

'I let her taste your fate.'

Hakon winced. 'You sold her into slavery?'

'She is *my* slave.'

Hakon blinked at his brother's possessive tone and Egill raised his brow pointedly, before saying, 'Yes, *his* slave… He even dragged her here with us. She is back on the ship, locked in the hold. She will be relieved to know you are alive. Grimr threatened to throw her in the sea if he found you dead.'

Hakon frowned. 'I hope you have not treated her badly. I think she might have even saved my life. Ingvar would have happily killed me, but she was the one to convince him otherwise.'

'I doubt she did it out of kindness!' Grimr's lip curled with disgust.

'Still… I am alive and well. It would be wrong of you to keep her as a thrall and continue her punishment.'

Grimr gave a light shrug. In Hakon's experience that was all his brother would say on the matter. He was tight-lipped when it came to apologies…and emotions.

Grimr despised betrayal above all things. As he had been the one to convince Hakon to agree to a marriage alliance initially, he would be doubly burdened by the guilt and responsibility of that mistake.

Eventually, Grimr said, 'She deserves worse than what I have given her. We heard how you were forced to marry a woman to regain your freedom. The blacksmith at the port said you were also dragged into a feud and that there was talk of a raid. So, we came as quickly as we could.'

'Thank you, your timing was fortunate indeed and I am glad to see you both—I take it your injuries have healed well?'

They nodded and Grimr said, 'There is much to tell you, about Ingvar and King Harald's demands—'

Hakon nodded, but raised a hand to silence his brother. 'Come inside, we have much to discuss.'

Chapter Thirteen

The brothers were an intimidating sight to Orla and the other women. They were not used to so many men in their household, let alone giants.

Most Norse men were big and broad, but these men were trained warriors and skilled leaders. They had grown up on rich meat and the best grain. They had not starved or struggled like many of the islanders had.

The hall was crowded with so many people that Orla felt as if she had invited an entire army into her home. Their presence worried her women and she wondered if she should move them into her chambers tonight. It would be crowded, but safe.

She turned to Mildritha as the woman put down a basket of bread in the centre of the table. 'Mildritha, tell the women to move their rolls into my chambers. Move furniture if need be. I want all the women in there tonight.'

Egill laughed. 'Your new wife does not trust us, Brother!' As Mildritha passed him he gave her a dazzling smile that caused her to blush furiously.

Orla felt a momentary pang of guilt that she did not trust the men who had saved them.

'I trust her decision more than I trust your ability to behave!' snapped Hakon in response, but she could tell he was only teasing and Egill's hearty laugh confirmed it, immediately easing her worries.

'Make way for my wife, she is the mistress of this hall, so show her some respect!' he added, shoving his brother to the side.

Orla squeezed in to sit beside her husband, grateful for his reminder regarding her status—when there were gods of war dominating your table it helped to have your position openly respected. The serving women seemed to relax, too, and they moved with more ease and confidence around the many men as they sat at their benches.

Grimr spoke loudly and with a firmness that demanded Hakon's attention. 'I killed Ingvar.'

Hakon smiled. 'That was quick! Thank you, it will save me the trouble of killing him myself.'

Orla's heart leapt in her throat. If Hakon's enemy was dead, would he stay in Iceland? It felt like a hopeless possibility and she clutched her hands under the table to stop them from shaking.

Grimr was not done. 'It does not solve our problems. If anything, it has made matters worse. King Harald is not pleased with our families' feud. He demands the alliance remain, otherwise Ingvar's and our supporters may clash in the future. He is worried it could break the unity of Norway.'

Hakon nodded. 'He will not allow that, not after fighting for so long to build it.'

Egill spoke next. 'King Harald ordered us to find you. He wants the marriage between yourself and Ingvar's sister to still take place.'

Orla's throat tightened painfully and tears pricked at the back of her eyes.

It was worse than she could have ever imagined!

She would lose Hakon in every way. Not only would he return to Norway as he had always planned, but he would be taking another woman as his wife. A powerful, Norse woman, who was the perfect match for a jarl...unlike Orla, a Celtic, former slave girl with no blood ties to speak of.

He would never come back.

'I am already married,' Hakon said and his brothers glanced at each other with confusion.

Egill was the first to speak. 'Harald has married several women to unify the kingdoms, he will not hold you to one match. Besides, a political alliance is different. Orla could come home with you—'

'I will not,' she replied sharply and Hakon's brothers stared at her in exasperation.

'The King's command was clear,' added Grimr.

'Orla is my wife. I will accept only her,' replied Hakon, and Orla's heart hammered in her chest.

Was he prepared to defy his King...for her?

It felt unreal.

'We cannot go against the King,' Egill said, for once a serious expression marring his jovial face. 'It would mean war.'

Unable to face another word, she rose from her seat and tried to appear as unemotional as possible, despite the fact her heart was breaking. 'Hakon.' He looked up at her with a pained expression, but when he opened his mouth to speak, she shook her head.

'You are a jarl of Norway, you should leave. I will not be the cause of any more bloodshed.' She glanced at Hakon's brothers, who seemed relieved by her words. 'Excuse me, I have lost my appetite.'

Orla walked into their bedchamber, the tears threatening to burst from her in a fountain of pain. Women were putting down bedrolls in her chamber and she was horrified to realise there would be witnesses to her misery. Their kindness would break her even more.

'Are you well, Mistress?' asked a concerned Wynflaed.

Orla struggled to hold back a sob as she gave a quick nod and hurried to the hot pool's door. 'I am fine. I need some fresh air, that's all, there is smoke in my eyes!'

Wynflaed hurried to light a torch and handed it to her. 'Of course, Mistress, take this. I will ensure no one disturbs you.'

Gratefully, Orla hurried down the tunnel, desperate to find some solitude where she could weep in peace.

Hakon strode down the black tunnel, more certain than ever about his fate. This time he would not leave it to the gods—he would grab it with both hands and refuse to let go.

When he emerged into the little hut on the other side, he saw the brazier had been lit—badly. It was only spluttering, a few flames dancing around the kindling as if Orla had not taken much care when lighting it.

His eyes searched for her. She was sat beside the hot pool, her back towards him, her feet dangling in the steaming water below. The moon above was large and bright, reflecting off the steaming water like liquid silver.

He reached into the brazier, moving one of the logs until the fire caught a little better. Then he moved towards her, only aware she was crying when he heard her struggling to sniff away her tears as he approached.

'I understand! There is no need to explain,' Orla cried, refusing to look up at him, her face turned away, her hair covering her face like a copper curtain. 'Go back, feast with your brothers.'

Kicking off his boots, he sat down beside her. Rolling up his trousers and taking off his socks, he dropped his feet into the water. Her legs were as pale as milk beside his, beautifully curved and elegant as they lightly dangled in the water.

'I cannot leave you. I swore an oath.'

'You must, otherwise you threaten war with your King.' She looked up at him then, tears shining in her swollen eyes, her cheeks and nose flushed from her crying. He smiled at the sight—she did everything with a fiery spirit, including weep. 'Forget your oath,' she said.

'I cannot.'

'Why? If it prevents war, then that is more important than some bargain you struck with me. Besides, you were a slave, you had no choice. The vow is meaningless.'

'Not to me.'

Orla gave a little scream of frustration and thumped

him in the arm with the back of her hand. 'Why are you being like this? You are a jarl. You heard what your brothers said, you cannot defy the King. So, go! Marry Ingvar's sister, make your King happy and give your people peace. That is what you wanted all along, is it not?'

'It was,' he admitted, smiling in amusement at her passionate declaration. 'But what do you want?'

'You have no need to worry about me. Skalla and Njal are dead, as is their power over me. No one will question or threaten it again…even…even if you never come back.' She turned away from him, choking on the last words as if they were too painful to speak. Her hand covered her mouth, trying and failing to smother her sobs.

He reached out and took her hand. Silver lines of tears glinted in the moonlight and he had never found her more beautiful—it pierced his side and stole his air.

He sucked in a painful breath. 'I agree, you will be fine here without me.'

She nodded quickly, clearing her throat. 'Ahem, yes, exactly.'

'But I will not,' he said firmly, his thumb brushing against her knuckles lightly. 'I cannot live without you, because I love you.'

Pain reflected in her eyes and she nodded. 'I love you, too, and it breaks my heart to let you go,' she whispered and his heart filled with joy. He couldn't stop grinning, even when she added, 'But, I must… My life is here.'

'Then I will stay.'

'But you cannot!' she cried, shaking her head vehemently, as she tried to tug her hand back from him.

He let go of her and her eyes widened with surprise as she rocked to the side. She pushed her hand down to stop herself from falling, but it was dark and she hit only air and then water as she fell into the pool.

A loud splash and her head went under. Rising moments later, she broke the surface, spluttering and shrieking through the steam indignantly, 'What did you do that for?'

'I didn't! You were the one who pulled away!' he argued, then with a laugh he dropped down into the pool beside her. The water was pleasantly hot, the stone beneath his feet warm. 'But wherever you go, I will follow.'

She swept back her hair and seemed to truly understand him for the first time. She stepped closer, resting her palms against his chest. 'What about the King?'

'He wants the jarl of my family to marry Ingvar's sister… That doesn't have to be me.' He cupped her face in his hands, brushing away the strands of wet hair that still clung to her cheeks, then dipped his head to kiss her mouth gently.

'You would give up your jarldom?' she whispered, her voice breathless with hope and longing.

He raised his head and drowned in her emerald eyes. 'I would give up Valhalla to stay by your side.'

Her smile was breathtaking and the pool suddenly felt uncomfortably hot, the wet clothes dragging against his body. He pulled off his tunic, then grabbed her by the waist, pulling her close.

This time when he kissed her, it was more urgent and demanding. She opened for him and softened against his embrace, willingly surrendering to his demands, while his fingers worked quickly, releasing the turtle brooches on her dress and absently dropping them on the stones beside the pool.

Orla parted from him for a moment, throwing off her apron dress and shift quickly, while Hakon removed his trousers.

'Grimr will not thank you, he seems to hate that poor woman,' Orla said and he could tell she was pitying them both.

Hakon smiled thoughtfully. 'She is the first woman I have seen Grimr obsess over... I think he likes her more than he cares to admit. Do not worry over either of them. Grimr is stubborn and awkward, but he has a relentlessly good heart...and, I think, so does Sigrid. They might make a fine match.'

Orla took a step closer and wrapped her arms around his neck. 'True... Convenient marriages can sometimes lead to deeper feelings.'

'They can.' He dipped down into the water, gathering her legs around his hips and then rising to carry her towards the opposite side of the pool, where he could see her body better beneath the moon.

Clinging to him, she began to press kisses against his lips and neck, rubbing against him like a cat, until he was rock-hard with desire.

Pressing her back against the side of the pool, he kissed her passionately, exploring and building the heat between them. Arching her back, she moaned as he consumed her with kiss and touch until all that remained was the need to unite.

She clung to his neck, curving her body against his, silently demanding he possess her in every way. Unable to deny her, or himself, a moment longer, he joined their bodies together, rocking into her and holding her tight as they moaned against each other's lips, sharing breath and incoherent vows of love beneath the immortal stars.

Hakon increased the pace, the water splashing around them as they made love. When they climaxed, she clung to him and buried her face in his neck. 'I do not deserve you,' she said and it broke his heart that she would think such a thing.

'I need you. I am afraid to live without you. You are the part of my soul that I never knew was lost.'

Orla looked up at him and they were so close he could feel the beat of her heart against the empty right side of his chest. He hoped she could feel his heart, too, in the space beside hers.

'I am so lucky,' she said with a soft smile.

Chapter Fourteen

Grimr was not happy about his new bride-to-be or title. He grumbled about it constantly, and tried to change Hakon's mind more than once. But his brother remained resolved in his decision. He would not leave Orla and he would not marry Sigrid.

'You will make a better jarl than I,' Hakon said over *dagmal* the next morning. 'You are more tactical in your choices and King Harald respects you.'

'He likes you more!' snapped Grimr and Hakon laughed at his brother's disgruntled tone.

'The King will not be concerned who marries Sigrid, only that the two families should unite. You can do that, I cannot.'

'You have condemned me to a deceitful witch!' snapped Grimr, although he could tell his brother was beginning to accept it.

'Would you rather Egill became jarl?' he asked and Egill spat out his porridge with a horrified expression.

To Egill's relief, Grimr grumbled, 'I may as well cast our family name into the sea if I did that!'

Egill nodded cheerfully. 'Very true, Brother. You do a great service for us by marrying her. It is not as if you had to shove her in the hold to stop yourself from staring at her all day and night.'

Hakon laughed as his brothers scowled at each other.

'Shouldn't you let her out of the hold?' asked Orla, concerned. 'She must be so confused and scared!'

'Why? She has plenty of food and water, as well as a guard to watch over her. She is fine and safer than if I'd brought her with me to battle.'

'But the poor thing has been aboard a ship for nearly two weeks! She must be desperate to step foot on dry land. You should stay a while.'

Grimr shrugged. 'No, we must go before the autumn storms get any worse. I plan to leave today…if all is well with you, Brother?'

Hakon nodded. 'Can either you or Egill return in the spring? I want to make a success of this land and could do with any supplies you might have spare.'

Egill cleared his throat, his eyes lingering on Mildritha as she walked among the tables. 'I think I will stay here for a while… I have a desire to farm.'

'Really?' Hakon said with a raised brow, then shrugged. 'I would appreciate your help. Once Skalla is buried, we will need to take stock of his land and goods. I could do with your charm and wisdom during the negotiations. Snorri has asked me to become a *godi*—one of the elders—which is fine as long as Orla keeps her vote within the assembly. They do not allow women to vote…but maybe you could help me persuade them to make an exception?'

Egill grinned. 'I would be happy to help.'

Grimr slung back his cup of water with a disgruntled growl. 'Then I must face King Harald alone. What did I do to deserve such disloyal brothers?'

Hakon slapped a hand on Grimr's shoulder. 'You are lucky, Brother, as am I!' He glanced at Orla and she blushed. He truly was grateful to have been her bought husband.

He reached for Egill, his arm crossing behind Orla's slim shoulders, including her in the embrace, as he proclaimed, 'No matter how far we are parted, we are family. One does not exist without the other.'

* * * * *

CHOSEN AS THE WARRIOR'S WIFE

Sarah Rodi

For Sue Merritt (Virginia Heath),
for all your encouragement and support

Dear Reader,

In *Chosen as the Warrior's Wife*, I was inspired by
the setting of the Eastern Roman Empire's capital,
Constantinople, where Viking warriors were hired to
fight and protect the emperor, and the sovereign's wife
was chosen from among the most beautiful Byzantine
maidens in a bride show. But it is the Viking who is the
hero of my story... Viking Fiske is bodyguard to the
emperor and commander of his Varangian Guard. He
and his men were hired to defend Constantinople—
and have succeeded. Fiske is set to be awarded great
riches, which he needs to gather an army of his own
to help him reclaim his place as ruler of Denmark. But
at the emperor's bride show, Fiske is given just half of
the silver he was promised and instead is told he can
choose a wife from among the women—their dowry
will be the other half of his reward. He chooses Kassia,
but his new bride keeps a terrible secret... Will they
find happiness in their marriage of convenience on
the dangerous road through the river rapids toward
Denmark? I hope you enjoy the setting and get swept
away in the romance like I did.

Prologue

Constantinople, 1035

Fiske lay on a bench in his longship in the balmy heat, looking up at the stars in the glittering night sky, listening to the sounds of celebration pealing out around the great city. It was a night to remember.

The capital was a captivating place, but Fiske had achieved what he had come here to do—the Emperor's kingdom was now secure—and he was ready to go home. He felt restless, for he had waited long enough to settle his own scores.

As chief commander of the Emperor's army, he and his men had been hired to lead the fight for Constantinople in battle after bloody battle these past five winters. They had been tasked with spending long, punishing years at war with each of the Emperor's enemies, crushing them one by one, and they had succeeded in suppressing the latest uprising within the city's own walls. His work here was done.

On the morrow, Fiske was to be awarded great riches

of silver and silk by Emperor Constantine, which meant he could finally return to Denmark with the means to reclaim his seat of power in Aarhus and avenge his father's death. He was eager to begin his journey and fulfil his destiny—to set sail for the north, back up the long and winding Dnieper, with his small contingent of men before winter arrived.

The sudden movement of his boat startled him, the harbour water gently lapping against the wood. Someone had stepped down into the hull, causing it to gently sway from side to side. He raised his head to see a cloaked silhouette bend over the prow and struggle with the rope tethering the vessel to the jetty. They cast it off and sank down on to a bench, their back towards him, but as they reached for an oar Fiske saw his opportunity. He was up on his feet, brandishing his sword against the thief's neck. They froze.

'*Stoova! Skelmir!* What do you think you're doing? You've picked the wrong ship to steal, *vargr*. Drop the oar and turn around. Slowly.'

Cautiously, the pilferer rose to their feet and turned. As their face came into the moonlight, he was shocked to discover it was a woman. A beautiful, but somewhat dishevelled woman, her cheeks marked with silvery streaks of tears. Tears that had left her ebony eyes shining—and now widened with fear.

An immediate slug of awareness took him by surprise. Never before had he hesitated when using his weapon, but seeing the sharp blade glinting against such beauty, he wavered for just a moment. He lowered the metal, moving it away from the perfect column of olive skin at her throat.

'Who are you?' she whispered, her chin tilting upwards, sounding more confident than she looked.

'Shouldn't I be asking you that question, given you were attempting to steal my ship?'

She furtively looked all about her, as if to check no one else was around—that she hadn't been followed—before glowering back at him. 'I thought everyone would be at the festivities tonight. I didn't think anyone would notice.'

'That doesn't explain it.' He took a commanding step towards her. 'Who are you and what are you doing on my boat?'

'I was just going to borrow it. I didn't think it would be missed—there are so many of them,' she said, lifting her hands up in exasperation.

'None like this one, which has travelled so far. It belonged to my father.' He remembered the man had spent weeks carefully carving the dragon head on the prow with pride. It had since allowed Fiske passage along the Silk Road to this land of riches and, for as long as he'd been in Constantinople, it had been his sanctuary when he needed to be alone. It had seen him through many storms and battles and, in a few days' time, it would be his means to get home.

She swallowed. 'I'm sorry,' she said, lowering her voice and the oar. 'But I need to leave the city.' She gestured to the majestic imperial buildings behind her. 'Tonight.' She sounded distraught—almost desperate. 'I'm sorry to disturb you. Now, if you'll excuse me I shall be on my way…'

His eyes narrowed on her and he sheathed his sword. 'If you're trying to make a quick getaway, stealing a boat really isn't the best way to do so,' he said, perversely not ready to let her out of his sight just yet, instinct telling him he needed to keep her talking.

What he should have done was throw her over his shoulder, carry her back to her home and not stop until he'd deposited her into the lap of her father—or husband. But something was holding him back. Right now, he had the feeling he was the only person who knew where she was. His interest had been piqued and he wanted to find out what she was planning.

'Whoever you're running from, you won't get far. You do know about the Great Chain guarding the way in and preventing ships from leaving the harbour? The Emperor's soldiers man these waters day and night.'

Her enchanting almond-shaped eyes darkened in anger. 'I think we are all well aware of his barbaric henchmen. We feel the oppressive weight of their tyranny every day,' she spat out.

He grimaced. For once, he was glad his uniform was covered by his cloak. She obviously didn't realise he was such a man.

'But I've made it this far—past the guards and beyond the city walls...'

It was no mean feat, he'd give her that. The massive fortifications were hard to slip in or out of unnoticed. His men must be celebrating hard.

'No one gets in or out of the harbour unseen. Besides, do you even know how to row?' he asked, placing his hands on his hips. 'I doubt you could handle this ship or the tides by yourself.'

She bit her lip, looking up the length of the boat and back at him, as if wondering what to do. 'Can you?' she asked hopefully. 'I will give you coinage for your silence and your help.'

'That depends.'

'On what?'

He crossed his arms over his chest. 'Who you are running from—or to?'

'That is none of your concern,' she said, pulling the hood of her cloak tighter around her, sending a delicate waft of alluring musk and mimosa his way.

'If you're asking me to involve myself in your situation, I'd say it is.' He leaned in closer. 'Are you on your way to meet a lover?'

'No!' she snapped and, curiously, her answer pleased him.

'Did you steal something—apart from attempting to take my boat, that is?'

'No!'

He stepped towards her. 'Are we to expect the Emperor's soldiers to appear at any moment?' Little did she know they were already here.

'I hope not.' She took another secretive glance all around them.

'Where is it you want to go?' he asked, staring down into her exquisite face. It was shaped like a diamond and she had high, sculpted cheekbones. She was clearly a native of this empire and he had never seen a more stunning creature. She was a dark, exotic beauty.

'Anywhere. Just as far away as you can get me.'

'Haven't warmed to the Grand City?'

'It's not the place, it's the people. Who *I* am here.'

He was struck by her honesty—that she would reveal such a truth to a stranger.

'People say in this city, you can be who you want to be…' After all, he had come here looking for fame and fortune and he had found it.

'Not so for me. It seems I can be only who others want me to be,' she said miserably.

'And who is that?'

She tossed her head and he saw a flash of her black, silky hair beneath her hood.

'Enough questions. I am in a hurry. What's your answer? Will you take me or not?'

The vision those words conjured up was certainly an inviting prospect and he felt a throb of unexpected desire. But he knew he couldn't do what she was asking, not unless she could wait a few more days.

'I do not need your coinage. And I'm concerned for your safety and your reputation, *kyria*,' he said, lowering his voice to a soft whisper. 'These dark waters are no place for a woman.'

She pulled back from him, angrily. 'So you won't help me?'

He realised it was too late anyway. In the distance, he saw a band of riders on horseback making their way along the shoreline. He felt sure they were heading in this direction. The sounds of the animals' hooves drew nearer, like the rattling beat of a warning drum.

'Kassia!' a voice raged.

Alarmed, she spun round and saw the men fast approaching. 'No!' she cried, horrified, shaking her head. 'It can't be.'

'Someone you know?' Fiske asked.

'My father,' she said in despair, batting away a frustrated tear.

There was no chance for her to run; the horses would be upon them in moments. She swiped off her hood, as if giving up her disguise, realising it was futile, and his breath caught. She was devastatingly beautiful.

As the riders bore down on them and the animals were reined to an abrupt stop at the end of the jetty, Fiske recognised the elderly leader, with a vein pulsing in his furrowed forehead, sweat on his swarthy skin, to be Governor Faustus. They had met on a few occasions in the Emperor's court.

'What do you think you're doing, you ungrateful, stubborn child?' Faustus bellowed. 'You will be present at the Emperor's bride show on the morrow, or you will bring shame upon your family's good name. Men, seize her!'

'No,' she whispered desperately, as his soldiers began to descend from their horses and move towards her.

Fiske saw her shoulders cave in, as if all hope was lost, and felt a pang of guilt that he couldn't help her. He at least wanted her to be spared punishment.

He stepped forward, blocking the soldiers' path. 'It's my fault, Governor Faustus,' he said, drawing a hand over his jaw.

The man swung to look at him—as did she—amazed. 'Your daughter wished to purchase a gift to present to the Emperor at the celebrations. Excuse all the secrecy, it was meant to be a surprise. I didn't mean for her to get into any trouble,' he said, declaring her innocent.

And to show he meant it, he reached inside his cloak and withdrew a small, bejewelled dagger and handed it to her.

Bewildered, maybe even a little suspicious, she closed her grip over the hilt and threw him a look.

'Is this true?' the governor asked his daughter.

Her beautiful brow creased. 'Yes, Father.'

The man nodded. Whatever he thought, he wouldn't dispute it now. He wouldn't argue with the Emperor's personal bodyguard. 'Then I thank you, Commander, for taking care of her. Kassia,' he said, in a warmer tone than before, 'let's get you home, Daughter. You have a big day ahead. You must get some sleep so you look your best.' He bowed his head at Fiske, who, in turn, inclined his own in acknowledgement.

Kassia went to scramble out of the boat and Fiske took her hand, helping her on to firm ground. He felt a spark of heat shoot through his arm at the contact. She glanced up at him, her eyes wide, as she stepped on to the jetty, her legs noticeably shaky.

'Stay safe, *kyria*,' he whispered.

Then she was hoisted up on to a soldier's saddle and they were gone, galloping away from him, heading back towards the imperial city walls and the imposing palace behind them.

Chapter One

Stepping out on to the platform in front of the bustling crowd, under the brightest blue sky, Kassia couldn't breathe. She was wrapped up in a swirl of tight golden silk, on show for everyone to assess. The grand stage was set against the backdrop of the Great Palace, its gleaming marble and colourful tiles shimmering in the scorching morning sun. She knew she was expected to look around in wonderment at the dazzling scene before her and feel lucky to be here, but she felt like screaming inside.

Her parents had told her over and again that she would be the envy of every woman, as this wasn't an auction at a bazaar—she had been chosen to be a participant in the Emperor's bride show, for which hundreds of people had travelled from far and wide to see.

It was tradition for the sovereign to pick a wife from the most beautiful women in the land and its neighbouring kingdoms, hand-picked by the royal mother. Refusal to comply would see her punished and Kassia's parents had made it clear from the outset they thought it was a great honour that she had been selected. They hoped she would be successful in attracting the Emperor's attention to secure their family's legacy.

Kassia did not.

She certainly didn't feel like one of the fortunate ones. She felt as if her life was ending. And she would never forgive her family for making her do this—for everything they had put her through these past few weeks.

She stole a look at the other participants—the eleven other noblemen's daughters in swathes of decadent silk and velvet—and pitied each and every one of them. Were they forced into this, too? Had they been poked, prodded and humiliated for weeks, pruned and groomed to look the part?

Now it was judgement day and as Kassia walked out across the sumptuous stage, decorative drapes gently floating in the warm breeze, tulip petals scattered beneath her feet, she forced herself to place one foot in front of the other. She tried to pin a smile on her fearful face as she neared the platform where the Emperor and his entourage were sitting.

If only that stranger hadn't thwarted her escape last night. If only he had accepted her coinage and taken her far, far away from here… She would have missed the vivid colours of the city, the fig forests and vivacious markets, but not the riots, rebellions and invasions that had ravaged the capital for years. And certainly not the people.

She felt the Emperor's beady stare rake over her body as she drew nearer and it made her shudder. She couldn't bring herself to look at him. Instead, sensing another pair of eyes on her, pulling her in their direction, she turned to focus on the guard next to Constantine and her stomach flipped. His intense, piercing gaze locked with hers across the platform and her perfectly practised steps faltered.

It was the man from the boat. The one from last night. What was he doing here? And at the Emperor's side? Her mouth dried. *Commander*, her father had called him...

Suddenly, she was glad of her veil, keeping her face somewhat obscured, yet she couldn't help but take another glance at him. He had momentarily stolen her attention. He had long, reddish-blond hair, pulled back in a band, and his hand held the hilt of his sword—the one he had threatened her with last night. She had sensed the power behind his tall, muscular frame when he'd stepped towards her in the dark, but in the daylight he looked even more impressive. He had a mighty frame and towered over the Emperor, a red ruby set in his left ear, and he wore the dragon emblem of...

Her mouth parted on a gasp. She couldn't believe it. He was a man of the pledge—a pagan mercenary. A member of the Varangian Guard.

These men were the sworn companions to Constantine, recruited from Denmark and Norway, known for their loyalty and brutality while carrying out the Emperor's most abominable orders. These men were monsters and feared by all...yet he had been merciful towards her last night, when he could have had her arrested for attempting to steal his boat! Instead, he had protected her from her father's wrath.

His eyes—as blue as the Bosporus Strait—did not move from hers and the prolonged contact sent a strange shiver of awareness down her back.

Scars criss-crossed over his left cheek and he had a prominent dimple in his chin—he was striking to look at.

The Emperor leaned towards him, speaking into his ear, and suddenly the moment was broken. Kassia was reminded of where she was and what she was doing here.

Her heart pounded, her body thrumming. Would the commander reveal to his ruler the details of their encounter last night and her attempt to flee the city? The Emperor would see it as an insult and she would undoubtedly be punished. But a prison cell—even death—might be preferable to this bride show, she thought.

She averted her gaze, telling herself to remain calm, and made her retreat to the side of the stage, taking her place in the line-up. She lifted her chin just a little bit higher, trying to focus on the tranquil water of the harbour in the distance, willing her mind, if not her body, away from here.

When all of the candidates had done a turn on the platform, to raucous applause from the crowds, the Emperor descended from his throne and asked each one of them to step forward for his assessment. Some were asked questions, others were commanded to showcase a talent. Kassia's skin prickled in disgust. She did not want to perform for him. She did not want his eyes or his hands on her, let alone want to converse with him, and that familiar, stomach-clenching dread gnawed through her.

'Remove your veil,' the Emperor barked, when it was her turn.

With trembling fingers, she lifted the tulle from her face. He took her chin between his thumb and forefinger and she flinched at his touch. He tilted her face up, moving it to the left and right, studying her features. And then he stepped back and allowed his gaze to roam leisurely over her body.

As if he could sense her discomfort, Constantine smirked and she felt the bile rise in her throat. She had never been so humiliated. She felt like the cattle taken to market. Did he not care to know the character of any of these women, or was their worth only to be measured by their beauty? Not for the first time, she cursed her good looks, wishing she had been born plain.

At least he seemed unaware of her misdeeds last night. The commander must have kept her secret. Why? It was strange…the man's actions seemed at odds with his reputation as a ruthless warrior. Still, she was grateful to him. And for the dagger he had given her last night. She was prepared to use it if she needed to.

She tried to stare straight ahead at a position just above the Emperor's right shoulder, until he moved on. She just wanted this to be over.

Fiske was astounded when the Emperor presented Anna, Princess of Kiev, with a golden apple, choosing her as his Queen. Constantine paraded her about, as if she were a pretty decoration on his arm, and the crowd went wild. Was it a political move to extend his control into Kievan Rus'? She would not have been *his* choice.

But he felt a strange sense of relief that Constantine had not picked the woman—Kassia—whom he had encountered last night. Was today's bride show the reason she had been trying to run away? If so, she must be the only woman in the land who didn't want to marry the Emperor.

'As her first duty as my bride, Princess Anna will now bestow my gratitude on my commander-in-chief and his men for crushing the latest uprising within these walls and making today possible…' the Emperor announced, addressing the people. 'Let his actions be a warning to you all, that any traitors will be crushed.'

Fiske made his way up to the platform and knelt before the Emperor and his chosen wife, before the princess motioned for a heavy chest to be brought out and set down before him. He nodded his thanks as she opened it. But when he saw the contents, his heart sank. It was full of silver, but it was half what they had agreed.

He rose to his feet in protest. 'Your Highness—'

The Emperor held up his hand to silence him. 'I know what you are going to say—that it isn't what we settled upon. But I have decided to give you something far greater than silver, Commander.'

Fiske's brow furrowed and he bit down on his cheek, his knuckles turning white around the hilt of his sword.

He knew he had to keep his anger in check. He could not make a scene right now.

'I am going to give you a gift—a souvenir, if you like—from my empire, to take home with you after five winters of service. A bride selected from the finest maidens in the land.'

Mutterings echoed around the crowd and Fiske felt simmering rage burn in his stomach. A bride could not buy his vengeance. He hadn't done the Emperor's dirty work for five winters to return home with a mere woman instead of silver.

'Each of these women bring with them an immense dowry,' Constantine continued. 'That will be the rest of your payment. And once you are wed, you will be aligned to our empire—an ally for all time, should I need to call upon you again. You will have a vested interest in these lands that goes beyond a cold transaction of silver.'

Fiske had not seen this coming and he guessed that neither had the remaining women, given their shocked cries as they looked between each other in horror, huddling close. He understood why. He was a Dane—a pagan in their eyes. They were here for the Emperor, not a hired barbarian. He was not a handsome man, like Constantine. He had scars carved into his face and body, and Danish blue ink etched into his skin. The Emperor had cheated them, as well as him.

'Your Highness, I cannot,' Fiske said.

'I insist. It would be insubordinate to decline my offer in front of all these people,' the Emperor replied, lowering his voice. 'Now make your choice.'

Fiske tried to swallow down his fury, his hands shaking with rage. He glanced around and saw the Emperor's native soldiers close in. He had to keep his control.

He wondered if the Emperor expected him to lash out... If Fiske reacted, Constantine would have an excuse to arrest him, or kill him—and wouldn't have to pay him at all. Was that what the Emperor was hoping for? To be rid of him now he had got what he wanted from him? The man's power was immeasurable, but Fiske was well aware he didn't always use it for good. He was as corrupt as most of the rulers he'd seen in his lifetime.

Thinking fast, he knew his options were limited. If he protested, he might be sent away empty-handed. At least this way, if he accepted, he could take half the silver he was promised. It might still be enough to raise an army of his own.

But marriage? He had never considered it. He didn't need a woman getting in the way of his destiny. He didn't want anyone depending on him. His path was already marked out. He had ambition far greater than a woman and a family. And yet...

He turned back to look at the line of women—or one, in particular. He hadn't been able to get Kassia's mesmerising dark eyes, stained with anguish and despair, out of his mind all night, or the nagging guilt that he hadn't been able to help her. And his desire had raged into the early hours, the hot and humid heat not helping. Never before had a woman made such a sudden, powerful impact. Looking at her now, she certainly shone brighter than silver. And she had asked him to take her far away from here. Perhaps she wouldn't be averse to the idea…

'I told you we harboured great riches, did I not?' The Emperor smirked.

'Indeed.'

'May I suggest Helene?' Constantine said, as he moved back towards the women, taking a brunette's arm and tugging her towards Fiske. 'She is very beautiful, is she not?'

The woman whimpered, her frightened face brought before him. Fiske did not want a wife who would cower from him. Yet he could tell the Emperor was getting cruel enjoyment from making the woman squirm.

'She is.'

But Fiske continued to walk right past her and instead halted before Kassia, her chin jutting upwards, her eyes staring straight ahead. A steely resolve seemed to have replaced the wretched hopelessness of the night before. She was the only one who enchanted him.

The Emperor sidled up beside him, a muscle flickering in his cheek. 'This is Kassia—"the Pure". A lot more wilful than the others.' He leaned in close to Fiske. 'I would advise against it…'

She had shiny dark hair that was bound up into an elaborate style, covered in a glittering headdress. Her jewel-encrusted tunic draped over the generous swells of her breasts and a delicate rope belt cinched in her waist, the tunic hugging the flare of her hips before gently cascading to rest on the ground. Elaborate, intricate Byzantine patterns and gems adorned the fabric. Fiske's mouth dried. The tunic alone was probably worth many ingots and yet he wondered at the real jewels that lay beneath. She was stunning.

'Move on, don't be too hasty. Have a good look while I meet my new bride's parents and discuss their most generous bride price that will greatly expand my empire.' The Emperor laughed gleefully.

But Fiske remained where he was.

He had watched in fascination as the twelve beauties had strutted down the stage in a lavish, decadent display. The women all wore extravagant, dramatic tunics of various colours, sparkling with jewels. It was a feast for the eyes. Yet never had he thought the Emperor would offer him one of them. He hadn't even considered marriage before this very moment. But looking down at Kassia, he had never been so tempted. He hadn't been able to take his eyes off her as she'd shimmered along the platform. There was something about her.

When the Emperor was gone, the other women saw their chance to retreat, backing away, leaving Fiske alone with Kassia. She lifted her face to look at him and their eyes clashed. He felt an unexpected clamouring in his chest, before she quickly averted her gaze. He took a step closer and she glanced back. Their eyes met again and he felt a connection between them he couldn't explain.

How could the Emperor not have chosen her for his bride? She was by far the most beautiful. She was the most exquisite woman he had ever seen.

And yet, it was her words from the night before and her actions that had truly made him take notice.

Wilful, the Emperor had said…

Somehow, he knew she wasn't like any other woman he'd ever met. She knew her own mind, had her own opinions and was determined to fight for them.

He leaned forward to whisper so only she could hear. 'Do you still need that boat ride out of here?'

'I'm afraid you're a day too late,' she said curtly. 'I needed your help *yesterday*…'

He gave a tight nod, taken aback by her hostility. 'I guess the need to leave may have dissipated now the Emperor has made his choice.' He took a step away. 'I hope things worked out the way you wanted them to.' He turned to go.

'Wait,' she said, reaching out and touching his forearm, shocking them both. He stared down at her delicate fingers curved over his inked skin. He had wanted her from the moment he'd seen her again—and her touch made his desire soar.

As if realising what she'd done, she snatched her hand back. Had she felt the sudden spark, too? Or had she just seen how it looked, given the situation, the many people watching from afar—as if they were already lovers?

'Actually,' she said slowly, lowering her voice, 'the need to leave may be greater than ever before.'

The sultry tone of her voice drew him in, yet his brow furrowed, wondering at her reasons. 'Then perhaps we can help each other?'

She swallowed. 'Perhaps…'

The weight of the decision hung before him, hot and heavy, and sweat licked his brow in the sticky morning heat. Could he really marry a woman he didn't even know because the Emperor had demanded him to do so?

And could he take her away from this gilded place and all its riches to an uncertain life back at home? She would be his responsibility. He didn't even know what he was returning to and there would be a great battle before his future could be determined. He might not defeat his uncle... Could he subject his bride to a life of danger if he were to fail? He felt a duty to warn her.

'I'm leaving this place. For good. I'm returning to Denmark and I won't be coming back. Think hard. Is that really what you want?'

'Yes,' she said slowly. 'It is.' She shook her head. 'But I don't even know your name!'

They both knew this was madness, yet he had wanted her from the moment he'd first seen her and, surprisingly, he was willing to go through with this based on the strength of his desire alone.

'Fiske.'

He watched as the shock and dawning realisation of who he was crossed her face.

'I have heard that name. You are a renowned warrior. The Fisherman—isn't that what they call you? A name that strikes fear into the heart of the people... I have heard stories of your many battles... How is it that you came to work for the Emperor, Commander Fiske?'

'I needed the silver.' He wanted to buy an army, to claim back something that was taken from him.

She frowned. 'And you're prepared to marry a woman you don't even know, just to achieve that goal?'

'If that is what it takes… Are *you* prepared to marry a man *you* don't even know, just to get away from here?' What was she running from, if it wasn't an unwanted, arranged marriage? he wondered.

She bit her plump bottom lip and his gaze was drawn to her mouth.

'It would need to be a marriage in name only.'

He tilted his head to the side, studying her, and felt his smile slowly build.

'I see.'

He knew what she was trying to say. She had no intention of taking their marriage any further than this convenient arrangement. But she was too beautiful for him to marry and not take to bed. It would be like being given a gift of an incredible stallion and never being able to ride it. He had already started imagining what it would be like to touch her, to kiss her…

He felt sure her reaction to him had been just as potent. He knew he hadn't misread the widening of her eyes or the rapid fluttering of her pulse at the base of her throat. But for whatever reason, she was trying to deny it.

'You might feel differently once you get to know me.' He grinned.

She shook her head, adamantly. 'I won't.'

His smile grew wider. He would just have to be persuasive and bring her round to his way of thinking after the ceremony was over. After all, he liked a challenge.

Chapter Two

'Are you coming?'

The sun was burning through the morning clouds and Kassia stood on the jetty where she had met her new husband just a few nights before.

Fiske was in the hull of his boat, dressed in a leather and chainmail vest and dark tunic, his sleeves rolled up, and his large, tanned hand was outstretched towards her. Flutters filled her chest and a strange, responsive heat burned low in her stomach. She could see the swirls of dark ink on his forearms, which both disturbed and intrigued her. Had she made the right decision?

A giant of a man, he had beautiful blue eyes she didn't want to look into—she might have second thoughts. And his smile was disarming—it had already had her agreeing to marry him on a whim. As for his extraordinarily strong body, she knew he would be able to overpower her if he wanted to—as well as the thirty or so men bustling around him, readying the boat to leave. She had brought her dagger, just in case.

Yet right from the outset, she had felt, deep in her gut, that he wouldn't hurt her. She could never have gone through with this otherwise.

They had been married swiftly and quietly in Nea Ekklesia church. She could see no greater revenge on her parents—and the Emperor—than agreeing to Commander Fiske's proposal.

Her mother had been outraged that Constantine hadn't chosen Kassia as his bride after the lengths to which they had gone to please him. And her father had been appalled, making his disgust clear that his daughter was to wed a hired pagan mercenary. But once Constantine had offered her and the other women up, and Fiske had made his choice, there was nothing anyone could do about it.

During the ceremony she and her new husband had both been crowned, as was tradition in Constantinople, naming them King and Queen of their home. The crowns symbolised martyrdom, since it was said every marriage involved sacrifice on both sides—yet she was filled with relief that this was the only crown she would ever wear, that she wasn't being wed to the Emperor, but instead escaping his clutches.

Fiske had made it known he wanted to set sail for Denmark as soon as possible, which aligned with her own desires to get away from this place. And he had agreed to her terms and seemed to be sticking to his word—they hadn't been alone once in days. Only looking up at him now, expectantly waiting for her to take his hand, she suddenly felt uncertain. She didn't know the heart of him.

She had always thought she would marry for love and have a family, not tie herself to a stranger. Yet there was something about him, her response to him, that was carrying her forward. The fact that he had protected her on the first night they had met made her think there was a warmth that belied his fierce reputation. She had decided she'd rather take her chances with him. She just wished she had some of his chainmail—it might make her feel stronger.

'Worried you can't handle the journey?' He grinned, gently mocking her hesitation.

'Of course not,' she said, accepting his challenge but ignoring his hand, instead lifting up the hem of her tunic and stepping down into the boat.

She didn't dare touch him, for every time she did, her body reacted peculiarly, sudden heat rippling up her arm. She didn't understand it. She had felt it the first night they had met, when he had helped her out of the boat, and during their wedding ceremony when his strong hands had been bound to hers. She could still feel the searing sensations now.

No, the journey she could handle. It was her new husband she was unsure of. It would be so much easier if he didn't look the way he did. Intense. Formidable. Fascinating…

A trickle of sweat licked at her back in the arid heat as she steadied herself in the vessel. She had never even been beyond the city walls before and now she was setting sail for another land entirely. She had longed to step beyond her father's control and explore new places, so it thrilled and terrified her in equal measure.

Fiske cast off the rope and motioned for her to sit in the middle of a bench. As the boat began to leave the shore, she waved to her mother and father. For the first time, they had been almost contrite as they had drawn her into a goodbye embrace with uncharacteristic affection. But they had brought this upon themselves, she thought fiercely, unwilling to forgive.

Would she ever see them again?

It was strange leaving them on the jetty, watching them get smaller and smaller, as if her problems were diminishing with every stroke of the oars.

'Are you all right?' Fiske said, moving around the vessel, tying trunks, reminding her of a new complication she had to deal with now. What if she had swapped one nightmare for another? What if she had married someone worse?

'Yes. I told you I was ready to leave.' She sniffed, crossing her arms over her chest.

'I know what it's like to part ways with family. My siblings will all be grown now. I think perhaps I will not recognise them, it's been so long.'

She knew he was trying to make conversation, perhaps to put her at ease, but she didn't really feel like talking. She wasn't ready to get to know him just yet. She had hoped to keep him at a distance.

She sighed. 'How long have you been away?'

'Five winters. Longer than I ever intended... The Emperor's work kept me here for many more moon cycles than I would have liked.'

He came to sit down beside her on the bench. He picked up an oar and began to row, his large muscles bunching as he moved his arms, perfectly coinciding with the rhythm of the others. She was excruciatingly aware of his proximity, his strong thighs and elbows almost brushing against her as he stroked the oar through the water, and her breathing halted. She tried to hold her body away from him.

'It is quite a while to be in the service of the Emperor. Of all the people you could serve, why him?'

'He was looking for recruits with ambition. I needed to make a name for myself.' He shrugged.

'By killing people?'

He slanted her a look. 'By ruling people, keeping order.'

'With fear.'

His eyes narrowed on her. 'I do not seem to scare you, else your tongue would not be so sharp.'

Surprisingly he didn't…but the way he made her feel did. It was terrifying. Was that why she was already sniping at him, trying to keep him at arm's length? In his company, she was suddenly so much more aware of everything. The sound of the sea birds squawking as they circled overhead. The rushing of the water as the boat sliced through it. His steady breathing.

She tried to distract herself by taking in their surroundings. They were already a fair distance from the shore, the men's powerful strokes meaning they were gliding along the smooth waters at quite a pace. They passed the protective city walls and the watchtower standing sentinel. She had never seen the landmarks from this perspective before, yet she could barely concentrate. The man beside her was frustratingly stealing her interest. She could feel his penetrating gaze beating down on her, hotter than the sun.

'What is your home like in Denmark?' she asked, curiosity getting the better of her.

'We have a settlement on the coast, just like you are accustomed to living by the sea. But our land is flat and green, unspoilt and rugged. Wild.' It was as if he was describing himself, she thought. 'There are no grand palaces and vibrant bazaars. I hope you will like it, as we all do.'

'You said you needed to get away to make a name for yourself…so what is it that you do when you're not fighting?'

'We work the land, manage our own crops and animals.'

She swung to look at him. 'You're a farmer?' she asked, surprised. 'So you came here to make your fortune and a better life for yourself?'

'Something like that.' He grimaced.

'You got what you came here for, then,' she said, motioning to the trunks filled with silver and jewels surrounding them.

'More than I hoped for, wouldn't you say?' he said, giving her a wink.

Her heart picked up speed.

'You desire to be rich?'

'The silver is just a necessity. I need to raise an army of my own—to take back something that was stolen from me.'

'What? What was stolen from you?' she said, leaning forward.

He made a few more strokes before letting out a heavy sigh and putting down the oar. 'When I was just a boy, of ten and four winters old, our settlement was attacked. I lost my home—my birthright. I vowed that one day, I would seek vengeance and reclaim my family seat—I just had no means to do it.'

She frowned. 'And now you do?'

'Yes.'

'So you are taking me from one land of disruption to another?'

'I came here to put out all the fires in your lands and succeeded. Fighting is just a means to an end. I want peace as much as anyone… Do you want to learn how to row?' he asked her, suddenly changing the subject and offering her a grin. 'You seemed keen the other night.'

She looked at him, shocked. Was he serious? Would he really share that knowledge with her—let her have a go? Growing up in Constantinople, women were rarely allowed to do such physical things and she had always felt it unfair. She had wanted to learn to ride like her brother, to gallop through the fields at one with the outdoors and be taught how to fight with a sword—not sit and do needlework.

'Do you think I'm incapable?'

'Not at all!'

'You're not mocking me?'

'No, I thought you might enjoy it.'

'All right.'

He nodded and then moved closer and, without warning, put his arm around her. Panic floored her and she froze in horror at his nearness.

'What are you doing?' she gasped in protest, her voice sounding strangled.

He must have seen her startled look, heard the alarm in her voice, and she hated that he would see she was afraid. But she couldn't help it.

'Relax, Kassia,' he soothed.

His large hands covered hers, firm but gentle, and wrapped her fingers around the narrow pole of wood, then he began to rotate their arms, showing her how to move the flat end of the oar through the water.

She couldn't breathe in his proximity. She could feel the heat radiating from his body, his skin brushing against hers, and she could smell his scent—a mixture of sea salt, warmth and spice. After a few strokes, she let go, breaking the connection.

'You have to hold it if you want to row,' he mocked.

'Maybe another day,' she said. 'I'm not really in the mood.'

He shrugged, accepting it, and let her go. 'So, are you going to tell me what you're running from? Now we're a safe distance from the capital, you can speak freely. Why didn't you want to marry the Emperor? Not impressed by *his* wealth and power?'

'No.'

'Want to tell me about it?'

She shook her head. 'I hate that man.'

The words Constantine had whispered to her just days before still taunted her, making her shudder.

'Strong feelings. Although men who abuse their position tend to have that effect. I often found his desire to dominate, his craving for absolute power, somewhat disturbing.'

She paled. It was exactly that. 'Yet still you chose to fight for him.'

His jaw hardened. 'I told you, a means to an end.' He picked up the oar, but he didn't start rowing again, too focused on their conversation. 'He chose another for his bride and you still wanted to leave. Why?'

She glanced around her, twisting her hands in her lap. She had needed to get far away, beyond the Emperor's reach. And it felt good to be putting distance between them. Yet she was aware Fiske was staring at her, with his intense, penetrating blue eyes, wanting answers, and she sighed. Was there any harm in telling him now?

'The Emperor told me if he didn't choose me to be his wife, he would still make me his mistress...'

Fiske studied her, allowing her words to sink in, and his face darkened, as if a cloud had passed over the sun. 'So that's why he was trying to convince me not to pick you. He wanted you for himself,' he said slowly, realisation dawning. 'I wondered why he hadn't chosen you—you were by far the most beautiful.'

She felt her face heat at the compliment, yet she also felt a spark of anger. 'I am more than a pretty face.'

'I'm sure you are,' he said. 'I'm just saying now it makes sense. He had planned to marry the woman who could expand his kingdom because he had thought he would make you his anyway. No doubt he wasn't too happy with my choice to make you mine, then.' He ran one of his hands over his hair. 'So what you're saying is, I saved you?' He grinned.

She felt a responsive whoosh in her stomach. He was heart-stoppingly attractive, yet his words about her being his made her feel as if she was a shiny object to own—mere chattel. It made her want to lash out.

'If you can call a forced marriage a rescue.'

A muscle flickered in his cheek and he dropped the oar. 'Forced? I thought we agreed it was mutually beneficial. You didn't have to agree to it.'

'Do you really think I would have said yes if there was another way out? Another option? You are a Norseman! I certainly wouldn't have married you by choice. And please don't insult me—don't pretend you married me for anything other than my dowry.'

'Any one of those women could have given me that.' He raised his hand, brushing his knuckles down her cheek. 'It wasn't them I desired.'

Her breath caught. 'We agreed this marriage would be platonic,' she said, turning her face, shrugging him off. She felt panic, and something else she didn't recognise, rising in her blood.

'No, you decided. No man in their right mind would marry a woman they weren't attracted to and didn't want to sleep with. You must know I want you in my bed, Kassia… I thought I could change your mind.'

She reeled, shaking him off, alarm tearing through her. Now she was afraid.

She was disturbed by his words, but equally shocked by the responsive heat rippling through her, caused by his touch. She didn't know how to deal with this. 'You don't even know me,' she spluttered.

'You're right. But I want to.'

'We had a deal.' She was aware her voice was sounding high-pitched—and breathless. 'What you're suggesting… That is one duty I will not perform!'

'Duty? It would be more about pleasure. Yours as well as mine.'

She stood abruptly, needing to get away from his heated, expressive eyes—and his disturbing touch. 'There would never be any enjoyment in it for me. You're a…a heathen!'

He reeled, as if winded, and she knew she'd hurt him. The warmth evaporated from his eyes. 'Sit down, Kassia,' he said, his voice stern. 'I don't want you falling overboard.'

She slumped back on to the bench, reluctantly. She smoothed her braided hair and took a breath. 'Can we not just accept that we used each other as a means to get out of a bad situation? But there is nothing else between us. In fact, it would be my preference if we made this journey in relative silence.'

'All the way to Denmark?' he mocked, raising his eyebrows.

'Is it so very far?'

He leaned in closer, bearing down on her. 'It's not so much the distance, but the terrain. First we have to go through the dark waters of the Black Sea, then up the uncompromising River Dnieper, where we have to navigate the narrow Krariyskaya crossing and the rapids. There, we'll be at the mercy of the Pechenegs— a violent, dangerous tribe from the east who raid on the river. If we survive all that, we then have to cross the Baltic towards home, held hostage to the tides and storms. *If* we make it back, it'll be cold—a winter unlike anything you've ever known. I should have perhaps warned you it's a perilous journey.'

'You're trying to frighten me,' Kassia said, tipping her chin up. She would not let him intimidate her.

'I told you the night we met these waters are no place for a lady. If you're having second thoughts, it's not too late to change your mind... Perhaps it would be better if I left you here. Put an end to this farce of a marriage.'

She shook her head stubbornly. 'I'm not going back there.'

He stood, dangerously towering over her, and cupped her chin in his hand. 'Then remember that I gave you a choice. No one is forcing you to do this.'

She had never seen a man look so intimidating, so strong. Her body trembled in response. Did he realise how formidable he was? And then a thought struck her.

'Why do they call you the Fisherman?' she asked, curiosity getting the better of her.

He smiled wryly. 'We all have bynames. Erik over there is the Skull-Splitter.' She turned and glanced over her shoulder at a huge bald man. He gave her a crooked smile. He looked as though he could wield an axe with no effort at all. 'And that over there is Arne the Ale Lover... I'm sure you can guess why.'

She frowned. 'So why the Fisherman?'

'Because I always catch my enemy. No one gets away from me—unless I let them, Kassia,' he said warningly. 'This is your last chance to get out of my boat, *kyria*. I'm willing to release you further upstream if that is what you want.'

She shook her head.

'So be it.'

But when he turned his back on her to walk to the far end of the ship and speak with his men in the Danish tongue, she wondered if she'd made the right choice. All of a sudden, she felt so very alone.

The weather turned in the afternoon, just as they reached the unforgiving waters of the Black Sea. Its dark colour matched Fiske's mood, the towering mountains on its constraining shores closing in on them, adding to his sense of foreboding. Of feeling trapped. What had he done? He should have taken half the silver and been done with Constantinople and all the riches it offered. He should have outright refused the Emperor's offer of a bride. Now, he was bound to her—a dark, sharp-tongued beauty who didn't even seem to like him. Those arms crossed over her chest weren't welcoming—in fact, they were like a shield wall, raised to keep him at bay. And he hadn't failed to notice she recoiled every time he tried to touch her.

Kassia had told him she didn't want him—in no uncertain terms. She had made it sound as if he'd forced her into this and, strangely, he felt wounded by her rejection. But he was a fool. She had laid down her terms and he'd accepted them—what made him think she would change her mind?

She didn't know him—as she'd said, he was a heathen in her eyes. She'd had this sprung upon her and hadn't even had time to get used to the idea. To be fair, he hadn't wanted to be wed either. Yet he had *wanted* her. He had hoped she might have felt the same attraction he had on first meeting her.

He rowed hard in unison beside his men, taking out his frustration on the pounding waves, hoping the rain would help to dampen his desire, because despite her insistence that their relationship was to be purely platonic, he was still feeling the pulse of attraction thrumming in his groin. Yet she didn't want them to talk, let alone touch. Did she not feel the searing heat when their hands brushed?

When the priest had pronounced them husband and wife in the church, he'd given her the briefest of kisses. Her breath against his cheek had felt like a warm whisper on the breeze and he'd wanted more. He'd wanted to strip her of all her jewels and white silk and get closer. It had taken all his restraint not to go to her room on their wedding night and claim what was rightfully his. But he was no brute, despite what she might think.

Instead, he'd had a restless night's sleep, torturously imagining what it would be like to take her pure and perfect body. He'd told himself to be patient, that it would only be a matter of time, but now it seemed his desire was one-sided and it was maddening. It was making him regret his decision. It would be unbearable being this close to her all the time and not able to take her in his arms and into his bed.

His red-hot anger and longing at her words of rejection made him row harder, faster, trying to get them out of this storm. Currently, his new wife was sitting clinging to the rope on the side of the boat, her knuckles turning white, her loosely braided hair and ridiculous purple silk tunic getting soaked by the spray from the ferocious waves. If she wanted to isolate herself, if she didn't want to speak to him or be near him, then fine. She could fend for herself.

One thing was for sure—she must really not have wanted to be Constantine's mistress. And he wondered—had he made himself her enemy by being a bodyguard of the Emperor? He reached up and felt the ruby stud in his ear. She had said she hated the man. He quickly removed the stone, a representation of his loyalty to the Byzantine throne, and threw it into one of the nearby trunks. Hopefully she'd come to discover *he* was nothing like that man.

She was taking a huge risk, to marry a man she didn't know and climb aboard a ship with thirty Danes, making a hazardous journey and leaving her life behind. It took some courage. He knew he'd been cruel, taunting her with the dangers that lay ahead when it was his role to reassure her, but he'd wanted to test her resolve. He needed her to be sure—to know what she was getting herself into.

He couldn't believe the bold-faced audacity of Constantine—to agree to marry the Princess of Kiev in front of all his subjects while already plotting to take a mistress. And yet, Kassia was temptation itself...

As he watched her struggle against the undulating sea, the waves flinging her slender body around, a strange feeling of possession and responsibility tore through him. He didn't want her to be cold or frightened—or hurt. She was his to look after now and he felt a pang of guilt for trying to scare her with details of the journey, in retaliation to her stern rebuff.

This was her first time at sea. She might genuinely be scared and he was ostracising her, leaving her alone. Her ebony eyes were wide and, as they searched out his across the hull of the boat, her vulnerability—and something else he couldn't name—punched him in the gut.

It was too powerful to be one-sided. Maybe, just maybe, her stubborn reluctance to talk to him, to touch him, had something to do with the attraction she also felt, but wanted to deny. After all, he had given her a get-out, told her she could get off the boat and she'd declined. She had chosen to stay with him.

Perhaps she was just afraid. He had that effect on people. Maybe he shouldn't give up hope just yet...

Never one to give up too easily, he set down his oar and headed over to her. He began to make a roof out of one of the woollen sails, protecting her a little from both the pounding rain and the sea spray.

'Better?' he asked.

She nodded, dithering and pale, and her beautiful black hair having come loose from her braids was now plastered to her head. 'Thank you.'

'Here,' he said, passing her a fur pelt from under one of the benches. 'You're soaked through. Put this on. We're going to have to get you some more appropriate clothes. You'll catch your death out here in those flimsy garments. The further north we go, the colder it's going to get. It won't rain like this for too much longer, though. We're almost round the western shore. It'll be calmer when we get to the mouth of the river.'

She nodded, but didn't speak, her lips pressed together as she wrapped the fur around her.

When they rose over the swell of another wave before plummeting back down, she squealed and he sat down beside her. He took her hand in his, wrapping his fingers around hers. 'Just hold on. I've got you. You're doing surprisingly well, if this is your first time in a boat?'

She nodded.

'Arne was sick the whole journey here five years ago!' He grinned. 'So you're doing better than him.'

She smiled weakly and, when another swell took hold, she gripped his fingers tightly.

'My father loved the sea. It was he who taught me to sail,' he said, trying to distract her from her fear.

'You didn't mention him before, when talking about your home earlier,' she muttered, her teeth chattering.

'He was killed when our settlement was attacked.'

She glanced at him. 'I'm sorry. Were you very close?'

His mother had spent a long time in mourning, for theirs had been a great love. They'd been destined to be together since they were children. They certainly hadn't married on a whim, as he had. He wondered what his mother would think of his new bride.

'Yes. As the eldest son, he spoilt me. Taught me everything I know.'

When his father died, his life was changed. Suddenly, he was responsible for his family. His people. And they were all homeless. Hunted. When he'd finally got them to safety and they'd started to build up a new settlement, he knew he couldn't stay.

It was his duty to seek out the men who killed their leader, avenge his death and take back what was his. But first he'd needed wealth. And a reputation to strike fear into the heart of his enemy. Now, if he intended to keep Kassia in the habit she'd been used to, if he wanted to reward all his men, he would have to take his birthright back soon.

Another wave took hold and her body was thrown against his, crushed into his side, and he swallowed down a groan. Her curves felt so soft pressed against him and he couldn't help wondering what it would be like to peel her sodden clothes off and pull her naked into his arms. He struggled to get his desire in check. How could he be feeling like this in these conditions?

He forced himself to keep talking. He needed the distraction as well as she did now. 'Were you not close to your parents, Kassia?'

'No, not really. Especially when they began to use me for their own gain. Growing up, I always came second to my brother. When he died of the fever, their attention turned to me. It was as if I only existed to benefit them. They were so eager for me to marry into royalty, not caring about my thoughts on the matter.'

He frowned. 'I'm sorry, too. About your brother. But did you not want to be Queen?'

'No. I have no need of fame. Of ruling others. I never craved the power or wealth that they did. It changes people.'

Interesting, he thought. She had a way of taking

him by surprise. His father had always taught him to be wary of men and women who would use him for who he was, setting their sights on his land and titles. Yet she wasn't interested. She could have been an empress, but she didn't want to be.

He thought perhaps he should really mention his own ambitions—she had a right to know who he was. She might have got out of the boat after all. But now wasn't the time, not when another wave came tumbling over the prow, breaking on top of them, causing her to cough and splutter.

'Are you all right?'

She nodded.

'I think you may have severely disappointed your parents when you said yes to marrying me, then—a heathen from the north,' he conceded good-humouredly, repeating her insult from earlier.

And she laughed, despite the storm and her wet clothes. 'They were horrified.'

'All part of your plan, I'm sure.' He winked.

But she sobered. 'I'm sorry. For what I said earlier. It was unfair of me…'

'I've been called worse.' He shrugged. 'But surely you didn't agree to come with me just to make them angry? Please tell me there was more to it than that.'

'I told you. I was desperate to get away from them all and suddenly you were there, offering me a way out.'

'So you thought marrying a total stranger and a long trip over the ocean, across enemy territory, was less of a danger?'

'Yes.'

'And they were your only reasons?'

She swallowed.

'Fiske. The river!' his man Erik called.

He looked up and saw the mouth of the Dnieper was in sight and knew the men would need his help to steer the boat out of the waves and into the estuary.

'Saved—for the moment,' he whispered to her, before bringing her hand up to his lips and kissing the back of it. Her eyes widened and he released her, straightening up, removing himself from the intimacy of their shelter.

He wanted to explore their conversation further and he didn't want to release her hand, but right now he had to concentrate. Once they were out of this storm and in the narrow waterway of the river, he and his men would need to find a place to portage before they hit the rapids and sharp granite rocks. He wondered how she'd feel about having to continue their journey on foot for a while. If it was just him and his men, he wouldn't be worried about the terrain—or the Pechenegs. But he had a wife to think about now.

Chapter Three

The moment the boat had veered into the river earlier today, they had been instantly protected from the storm. It had still rained and rained, but there were no more waves to unsettle them. And no more need for a warrior with brilliant blue eyes to hold her hand.

When they finally came to a stop a while later, Kassia let out a huge breath. Pulling back the material of the shelter Fiske had made for her, she saw the men were hurriedly unloading all the trunks in the dwindling daylight.

Unfurling herself from her sodden, crumpled position in the hull, she felt awkward among all the activity, as if she was in the way. She struggled to pick up one of the boxes, wanting to show she could be helpful.

'I can do that,' Fiske said, moving to take it off her.

'There you go, thinking me incapable again,' she snapped, holding on to it. 'What's happening?' she asked. 'Why are we unloading—rushing?'

'We need to get out and walk for a while.'

'Walk?'

He pointed up the high forested hills and rocky cliffs. 'More of a hike, I'm afraid.'

'Up there? Now? But it's almost dark.'

'We can't stay here,' he said, helping her out of the hull just before his men hoisted the ship out of the water. 'This is known for being a Pecheneg area. They could attack at any moment and with the silver and jewels on board—and a woman in our midst—we would be quite a find. Come on,' he said, gripping her elbow, propelling her forward. 'Stay close.'

She tugged herself out of his grasp. 'Don't touch me!' She stamped her foot. Every time he did, he set her body alight. How had she thought she could ever be at ease in his company? He was overbearing. Maddening! 'I'm hungry. It's dark. I don't want to walk up a mountain. And you don't need to put your hands on me all the time! You have no right.'

He placed his hands on his hips, raising his eyebrows.

Actually, he had every right...

She gulped.

'Did you just stamp your foot at me?' he asked. And then he threw his head back and laughed, startling her.

Her stomach flipped. He was spectacular when he smiled. He took her breath away. 'What is so funny?'

'You are. You're out here, in the wild, with all these men, in hostile waters, and *still* you don't seem to see the danger at all.'

She did. She felt it every time he came near her. She was terrified of the way he made her feel.

'I don't appreciate you laughing at me.'

He straightened and stepped towards her. 'And I don't appreciate you arguing with me, disobeying my orders at every turn,' he said, reprimanding her. 'I'm your husband and you will do exactly what I say to keep you safe.'

Her husband...

She still couldn't believe it. She was married to this man! She was his and he was hers... His words sent a strange tingle down her spine.

'And if you don't start walking right now, I'll just have to throw you over my shoulder and carry you!'

She had no choice. She put one weary foot in front of the other and began to follow the men carrying the boat up the well-trodden path. She tried to focus on the birds singing in the tall trees, the last of the daylight dappling through the leaves allowing them to find their way, and she noticed the sound of the tumbling water was getting fainter.

Fiske was right behind her and she wondered how she could be so aware of his nearness—even earlier when she'd been fearful for her life during the storm. She was grateful he had come over. She had been clinging on to the ship for dear life. But the moment he'd wrapped his fingers around hers, she had felt better. It was as if he was letting her know that, despite the unkind things she had said, he wasn't going to let her fall overboard into the ocean.

He was trying hard, she realised, attempting to put her at ease in this strange situation. And when her body had been thrown against his, she'd been disturbed that she'd wanted to lean further into him, seeking more of his comfort and protection. Surely she should be repulsed? She had vowed she would never want a man to touch her...

It felt as if they'd been walking for hours, her damp tunic swishing around her weary legs, her feet sore, when they finally came upon a rocky outcrop, surrounded by tall pine trees. The views were incredible of the ravine down below, showing them just how far they'd climbed, the last slither of sun and its golden warmth setting in the distance. She almost wilted with relief when Fiske said they should make camp there for the night.

He instructed the men not to light a fire, as they didn't want to draw attention to their whereabouts, but she was glad when they erected some small tents. She longed to put her head down some place dry— preferably away from everyone else. She felt tense from being in Fiske's company all day and longed to be alone.

They ate a meal of cold meat and bread, a few of the men telling stories of their battles. When the talk turned to their women, Fiske caught her gaze. 'You must be tired. Come on, I'll show you where you'll be sleeping,' he said, inclining his head in the direction of the shelters.

He led her inside a tent where his men had laid out a pile of furs. It looked inviting and she wanted him to go so she could collapse into them, curl up and go to sleep, yet he was showing no signs of leaving.

'Thank you. You can leave now.'

He grinned. 'You expect me to sleep outside with my men, instead of in here with my wife? No! Whatever would they think?' he said, his eyes twinkling.

She bristled. 'I don't care what they think!'

'I do. Their respect means everything to me. Do you think they'll look up to a man, follow him as their leader, if he can't even get his wife under control?' He stepped towards her, as if to demonstrate his power.

'Is that what you want? Me under your control? So you're going to go against your word. You're going to force me to do this?' She felt her knees tremble just a little, but tilted her chin up in defiance.

He clicked his tongue, making a disgusted tutting sound. 'I would never force a woman.'

She released a breath. She didn't know why, but she believed him. She had trusted him from the moment she'd met him, somehow knowing she would be safe with him. But he still wasn't showing any signs of going.

'Out of interest, why are you so reluctant?' he asked, stepping closer. 'We *are* husband and wife. We wouldn't be doing anything wrong.' He placed his hand on the wooden beam above her head, crowding her. Poles she thought she could use against him, if she needed to.

'I just don't want to.'

He brought his other hand up to stroke her cheek and she turned her face away, panic and what felt like the onset of a fever lashing through her.

He moved his hand away and rubbed the back of his neck, sighing. 'Very well. I promise not to touch you until you're ready, *kyria*.'

'I told you I will never be ready!' she said, looking

up at him, crossing her arms over her chest, trying to stand her ground. She didn't owe him anything. He had earned a great dowry from marrying her—silver that was meant to pay for her living in his home. She had laid down the rules of their engagement and he had agreed—it was he who was trying to break the terms. So why did she feel so wretched?

He shrugged and sat down on the furs. 'You keep telling yourself that, Kassia.' He grinned and began to tug off his boots. 'You might even start to believe it, even if I don't. But in the meantime, we *are* sharing this tent.'

He lay down on the furs, his hands crossed across his chest, his one long leg crossed over the other, and he closed his eyes.

Argh! He was aggravating! Infuriating! Staring down at him, looking so relaxed, she didn't know what to do with him. Should she leave and find somewhere else to sleep? She cautiously opened the door of the tent and saw some of the men asleep on the ground. She could hear them softly snoring. No, as much as she hated to admit it, she was probably safer in here with Fiske.

Frustrated, she slumped down on to the furs and curled up, as far away from him as possible, turning her back on him. But despite being exhausted, sleep eluded her. She tossed and turned, but no matter how much she tried, every time she shut her eyes, she saw Fiske's handsome, grinning face before her, offering her a mocking look, as if he knew she was lying to herself as well as him. As if he knew she was a coward—too scared to admit the truth of what she was feeling. But how could she? She didn't even understand it herself.

All their conversations since the first night they had met ran through her mind. She had answered all his questions honestly—until now. Even when she had told him she had never wanted to be Queen, it had been the truth. She had noticed his hands had tightened on the oar, his body had tensed—and she wondered if perhaps he thought she was lying, but she hadn't been.

She really had never craved power, only the autonomy of her own life. But now she felt as if she had lied because she thought perhaps she might desire him… It would certainly explain her reaction to him whenever he came near. Why she felt the need to push him away…and why she couldn't sleep now.

She sighed. She had treated him pretty badly today, calling him a heathen and saying she had been forced into marrying him. That she'd had no other choice. Because it had been her decision as well. She thought he probably deserved to know she had *wanted* to go with him. Could those words—instead of actions—perhaps satisfy him for now?

Frustrated, she pushed herself off the furs, sitting upright. She pulled the bands out of her hair and shook it free. She stole a look at him. Was he asleep? How could he be? Was he not as aware of her as she was of him? She knew she wouldn't be able to drift off tonight, not with him stretched out beside her. She tucked her knees up to her chin and drove her hands into her hair.

'Can't sleep?' he asked, startling her.

'No.'

'Why not?'

She shrugged. 'Perhaps because I'm not used to a man lying right beside me!' And then she relented. 'And… and because I'm feeling bad, for the way I'm behaving.'

He raised his eyebrows.

It was true, she was sorry. She didn't like the way she kept lashing out at him, being cruel—when he'd done nothing but protect her since they'd met. She didn't like herself very much and that was the very reason she'd left Constantinople. She hadn't liked who she'd become there—she had left to start anew.

'I want you to know I am grateful to you for taking me away from Constantinople.'

'I don't want you to be grateful, Kassia.'

'No, you want me to be willing.'

'That's not it either. I want you to be truthful…' he said, sitting up to join her in the middle of the furs.

Her breath hitched.

'I want to know why you really came with me. No more excuses.'

'I'm not sure I can explain it.'

He raised his hand to tuck her hair behind her ears. His blue eyes glittered down at her, his warm breath fluttering across her forehead. 'Try.'

'When I saw you again at the bride show, after you had helped me with my father, it felt as if we were being brought together for a reason. So we could help each other.'

'Is that all?'

She swallowed. 'No…'

His eyes burned down into hers.

'The truth is…I wanted to come with you. Please don't ask me to put into words my reasons, because I can't. It was just a feeling… An instinct.'

'Towards me?'

'Yes!' she said, exasperated.

His lips curved up into a slow smile. 'I think that's the most honest thing you've said since we met.'

'I'm glad I amuse you.' She licked her lips. 'Do you think it was easy for me, to come away with you and your men? It wasn't. And I'm afraid! Of being out here. Of where we're going. But mostly I'm just afraid of you and…and the way you make me feel.'

He cupped her chin with his hand, lifting her gaze to meet his. 'And how is that?' He seemed unwavering in his resolve to get answers, as if he was looking right into her soul.

She bit her lip, shaking her head.

He shifted on the furs, moving closer, holding her face in both of his hands, his thumbs circling the corners of her mouth. 'What are you feeling, right now?'

'Terrified. And unable to sleep.'

He grinned. His hand trailed down her arm and found her hand and his fingers entwined with hers. 'There is nothing to be scared of, Kassia.'

There was everything to be afraid of! She knew that more than most. Especially now she had revealed her attraction. She felt exposed. Vulnerable. She might have said the words out loud, but she wasn't sure she was ready to act on her feelings.

'Do you trust me, Kassia?'

'I don't know you!'

'But you want to?'

She nodded, biting her lip.

'Then I promise you this. I won't do anything you don't want me to do. Good enough?'

She nodded.

'Have you ever been kissed before?'

'No.' It wasn't a lie, but she knew she was allowing him to believe an untruth.

'Maybe that would be a good place to start?' he murmured, looking at her lips.

She shook her head.

'It's just a kiss, Kassia. That's all.'

Just...

Her gaze dropped to his lips. Her body was thrumming with panic and wild excitement.

He brought his hand back up to her cheek. He was so assured and she felt anything but. He ran his thumb over the curve of her lips and she quivered, holding her breath. He was so close she could feel his heat, his warm breath mingling with hers. Was he waiting for her to stop him? Should she?

Then he leaned in and she let her eyelids flutter shut as he carefully pressed his lips to one corner of her mouth and then the other one, before kissing her, softly, in the middle of her lips. He was gentler than she'd imagined a man such as he could be—his touch at odds with his hard body. There was something so controlled about him that reassured her and she found herself lifting her face, wanting more, allowing him to gently, tenderly, coax her lips open with his own.

She let out a little gasp, allowing his tongue to sweep silkily inside and her whole body trembled. It felt sensual. It was everything she wanted it to be—everything she'd always dreamed it would be—and amazingly, she felt herself responding, tentatively touching his tongue with her own, as his one hand stole slowly into her hair at her temple, holding her to him, as he drew her body closer into his arms.

She let her hands drift up to his shoulders, holding on, one hand sliding up to hold his jaw, courageously letting him know that she desired him as he did her.

He finished the kiss and stared down at her, his eyes raking over her face, her breathing erratic. 'Was that so bad?'

She shook her head, looking into his eyes. And then his lips were back on hers, kissing her again, and it felt glorious.

He broke away and began to leave a burning trail of kisses along her jaw, her throat, his hand sliding down her back, pressing her soft curves against his hard chest, binding her to him, and her head tipped back.

He gently lowered her down, pressing her back into the furs, and his kisses became more passionate, deeper than before. But when his body came over hers, crushing her breasts against his chest, she froze. This didn't feel like just a kiss, this felt like so much more!

She pushed at his chest, breaking their connection as she tore her mouth away from his. 'Stop!' she cried, staring up at him, stricken. 'Please. You said you wouldn't do anything I didn't want to do!'

He instantly lifted himself off her, dazed, as his

eyes blazed down into her eyes. 'I'm just kissing you, Kassia. Nothing more.'

Was it just she who had been falling into a dizzy spiral of need, drowning in desire? Suddenly it had felt too intimate and she'd panicked, needing to get away as dark memories mocked her. 'I can't do this,' she said, pushing at his chest, scuttling out from underneath him, folding herself up away from him on the furs.

He raked his hand through his hair, blowing out a breath, as if trying to rein in his control. Was his patience waning? If so, she couldn't blame him. She knew she was giving out mixed signals. Most men wouldn't stand for it. Most men would have taken what they wanted by now.

'What's wrong? You didn't like it?'

She shook her head. 'It's not that.'

'What then?'

She shook her head miserably. She couldn't look at him. 'I just don't think I can do this.'

'Can you at least tell me why?'

'It's the Emperor…' she blurted out.

Fiske's brow furrowed. 'What about him?'

Kassia wrapped her arms around her knees.

'He…' She swallowed. This was harder than she thought. It was as if her throat was closing up, preventing the words from escaping. She felt so ashamed. But she knew she needed to tell him. She couldn't keep it bottled up for ever. Especially when it was preventing her from even letting her husband kiss her.

'Kassia?' He reached over and took her chin in his hand and turned her to face him. 'Just tell me.'

She scrunched her eyes up and blurted it out. 'He demanded a night with me before the bride show.'

She heard his sharp intake of breath, confirming it was as bad as she knew it to be, and felt her stomach churn in response. She slowly opened her eyes and he lanced her with his.

'What?'

Her whole body trembled. Perhaps she shouldn't have said anything. But she didn't know how she could let him touch her, how he could understand her doubts and be as gentle as she needed him to be, if she didn't explain. And it was threatening to eat her up inside. She needed to tell someone.

'Tell me you didn't agree.' His voice was deadly, as if he was a different man to the one who'd been kissing her tenderly just moments before.

'My parents insisted I go to him.'

He cursed, turning away from her, rising off the furs, getting to his feet. He looked disgusted—with her, or them, she wasn't sure. Maybe both. And she felt bereft.

He stood like that for a while, his back towards her, before he raked his hand through his hair and turned round, his hands on his hips.

'Tell me nothing happened. Tell me you didn't want that.'

'Never!' she said violently, rising up on to her knees. 'You know I loathe him. I did not have a choice.'

'He forced you?' Visions of Constantine lifting her tunic as she stood there trembling, terrified, unsure what was expected of her, flooded her mind and a tear slid down her cheek.

'Yes… I don't know,' she said, shaking her head. She couldn't be sure. For how could she put all the blame on the Emperor? Although she hadn't wanted to do it, she had accepted his invitation and gone to his quarters, hadn't she? She had gone against her gut instinct.

Even now, she couldn't believe that her parents had made her go, despite her protests. They had been given a taste of the Emperor's generosity and good favour—and had wanted more. He had convinced them he needed to spend more time with her before the bride show, to get to know her better, and they had made her feel as if she should be grateful…that his attention was an honour and his advances should be encouraged. She didn't think she could ever forgive them for it. Or herself.

'You enjoyed each other?' Fiske spat out.

'No! There was no enjoyment on my part!' she said, anguished.

'So I sold him my sword and you sold him your body,' he said, shaking his head.

She felt sick at hearing his words. It made her feel like a whore.

'I gave that man five winters of my life—and now I want to kill him.'

As did she. Constantine had pushed her down on to the bed on her belly, with no words of devotion or care for her feelings. He had taken her as if it was his right. As if she had no control over her own body. And it had been agony. Afterwards, when he was done, he had dropped his tunic and left the room, while she had lain there, sobbing. After a long while, when she had realised he wasn't coming back, she had found her own way home, feeling utterly used.

She had not seen him again until the rehearsal a few days later, when she had looked at the other eleven women and wondered if they had each had to succumb to his advances as well. She had felt like a shadow of her former self. And when he had whispered in her ear his plans for them to be together, no matter what, making her skin crawl, she had known she had to leave. She couldn't face having his hands on her again.

Fiske loomed over her, the cool reproach in his icy gaze making her shiver. 'He told me that your virtue was intact.'

'His word cannot be trusted.'

His eyes narrowed. 'Nor yours either, it seems.'

She drew in a sharp breath. 'I have not lied to you.' Her worst fear was happening. She had told the truth and he didn't believe her. He was rejecting her.

'You weren't exactly honest either.' She felt the censure in his eyes. 'You should have told me, before we wed, that you are impure. In my country, there are conditions of honour. The gods will not look favourably upon us now.'

Then his eyes clouded over, a thought dawning on him. He stepped towards her. 'Could you...? Is it possible you could be with child?' He looked suddenly ill.

Her eyes widened and she felt her face drain of blood. 'What?' she whispered.

There was a terrible silence as his words sank in.

'You *have* been taught how these things work?' He scowled, furious.

Her hand came up to her mouth. 'Yes…' she said, afflicted. But she hadn't even thought of the possibility. She had been so disgusted by what had happened, so desperate to get away from that man, she hadn't thought of any consequences. Her heart began to thud in her chest. But a child was a gift given to those who were married, wasn't it? A gift to those in love?

And then his tone became icy cold. 'Is *that* why you agreed to marry me? A Dane, who lives far away from Constantinople—the only man who could rescue you from certain disownment and disgrace if word got out that you'd had sex out of wedlock? Tell me, is that why you let me kiss you tonight? Were you hoping to sleep with me and then let me believe it was my child? Was this all part of your plan?' His accusatory tone was like a knife to her heart.

'No!' she cried, appalled, her hand covering her chest. She felt ill. 'I would never—' She shook her head, vehemently. The tent began to spin slightly, as she suddenly felt light-headed, slumping down on to the furs.

He shook his head. 'Did everyone know? Was everyone laughing at me?' He seemed furious at the thought that the Emperor or anyone else had taken him for a fool. 'Well, my eyes are wide open now. I can see what a mistake I've made.' His face was grim and those beautiful blue eyes were filled with disgust—and regret. 'You've got your wish, Kassia. You can be certain I won't ever touch you again. I don't want you now.'

Chapter Four

Fiske's mood was worse than she could have imagined the next day. He was like the snow-capped fiery mountain in the east, boiling anger bubbling beneath the cold exterior. He couldn't even look at her, let alone speak to her.

Even his men were wary—she could tell they were being cautious, careful not to irritate him in any way in case his rage should be unleashed in a mighty eruption. She wondered at the respect he commanded—it was clear they all looked up to him, fought for him and would lay down their lives for him.

He had led a great army in Constantinople and had been successful in crushing Constantine's enemies and restoring order. She had heard of his brutality on the battlefield, yet that side of him seemed at odds with the way he had treated her so far. Apart from giving her the silent treatment today.

She wondered how he would adapt to being just a farmer when he returned home.

They had packed up camp quickly this morning and

they'd been walking ever since. She never thought she'd want to be back in that boat, at the mercy of the water, but her feet were burning and her legs weary, and she longed for sight of the river again. The route they'd taken was brutally long—had he taken it on purpose, to punish her? Her tunic was covered in mud, the material torn in parts from wading through bracken and branches, and she wondered what her parents would think if they could see her now. She was a state!

Fiske's cool detachment was maddening. She hated the thought of him thinking ill of her—that she'd somehow tricked him. Like his men who sought out his judgement, his good opinion of her meant a lot and pain sliced through her at remembering his harsh words, telling her he'd made a mistake in marrying her. She felt truly forlorn. Almost hysterical. Especially when her lips could still taste his potent kisses from last night.

Encased in his muscled arms, his tongue tenderly stroking hers, she had been surprised her body had come to life. She had begun to hope, to wonder, if she had been fortunate in her choice of husband—to find someone she desired and admired. But almost as soon as it had started, it was over. She had ruined everything by pushing him away and revealing what had happened to her at home. He had said he didn't want her now and she couldn't blame him.

When she thought about what he'd said about her being with child, she went cold all over. Was it possible? She hoped not. It would ruin her. And them, if she hadn't already crushed whatever spark had been lit between them when he'd kissed her last night. Now there was this void between them and she didn't know how to breach it—especially if he wouldn't even talk to her.

By nightfall, when they set up camp again, she felt desperate. He hadn't said one word to her all day and she was starting to get angry, rather than upset. When she saw him take one of the trails through the forest, she seized her chance to speak to him alone and followed him. He stopped to chop up branches of a fallen tree trunk—for firewood or maybe even to vent his frustration—finally allowing her to catch up to him.

'Fiske?'

He kept hacking at the wood and she found his indifference infuriating. She'd rather his scorn or his harsh words to this. Rage propelled her forward.

'Fiske.' She grabbed his arm, pulling him backwards. 'What—are you just going to ignore me now?'

'I'm busy,' he snapped, shrugging her off. He couldn't even bring himself to look at her and she couldn't bear it.

She gripped the handle of his axe and ran her fingers over the blade to stall him. She knew he wouldn't move it with her fingers wrapped around it. She knew he wouldn't hurt her.

'*Helvete!* What are you doing, Kassia?'

'I want you to listen to me.'

'Take your fingers off the blade.'

'Only if you'll hear me out…'

His jaw worked, but he gave a curt nod, reluctantly. She lowered her hand from the metal.

'I understand why you're upset. And I'm sorry I didn't tell you about what happened before now. It was wrong of me, I should have. You should have had all the facts before you married me. But I was ashamed. Why would I want anyone to know that it happened? I thought you might think I'd encouraged it, that I brought it on myself. And you did… But can't you see it was also irrelevant? Nothing was ever meant to happen between you and me… You accepted my terms—you agreed this would be a marriage in name only—and yet now you seem to care whether or not I'm pure.'

'I told you of my desire for you.'

'And don't you see why that might have unsettled me—after what the Emperor had done?'

Fiske let out a violent curse as if the very thought of it appalled him and he dropped his axe to the ground.

But she continued. 'Yes, I went to his quarters, but it was not willingly. I did not know what was expected of me. And I did not want him to do the things that he did. I begged him not to, but he thought he had a right over my body. Now it seems you do, too!'

His brow knitted together. 'We are husband and wife!' he said. 'And I have not and will not ever use force.' He raked his hand through his hair. 'But is it so wrong of me to desire you? And to have thought you were chaste? To want to know I'm the only one you've laid with?'

'Have *you* not been with another woman?'

'That is different.'

'No. The only thing that's different is I didn't give

my body willingly. There was no pleasure in it. It hurt,' she spat out.

Anger clouded his features again and he turned away from her. It was as if the very thought of it disgusted him, made him appalled, just as it did her.

She took a step towards him and bravely placed her hand on his shoulder.

'I'm sorry. I didn't want to keep it hidden from you. And I never even considered the fact I could be…with child.' She took a breath, apprehension swirling inside her. 'If I had thought I could be, I wouldn't have agreed to marry you. I know that would not be fair. I never knew such things were possible out of wedlock.' She felt so worked up. 'And I hope to God it isn't the case. If it is, I will beg you to cut it out of me because I could not live with myself, knowing I was carrying that man's child.'

Fiske felt shaken, stunned. He was in turmoil. The feelings raging inside him had been tearing him up all day. He had never been so angry with himself. He had never questioned his decisions before, but now he was wondering how he could have been such a fool, to marry a woman he didn't even know. Was she right— had he put her beauty and his desire to claim her above all else, like the Emperor? If so, then this was his comeuppance.

Betrayal had ripped through him last night. The feeling was nothing new—he had lived with it his whole life, since his uncle had turned on them all, killing his father and stealing their home and titles. But he never thought he would be betrayed by his own wife, so soon into their marriage. He didn't need someone else in his life he couldn't trust. But worse than doubting her, it made him doubt his judgement.

Kassia had gone to bed with the Emperor and the thought sickened him. He had thought she was his. Thoughts of that man taking her—and thoughts of the Emperor laughing at him—made his nostrils flare. That man had cheated him out of half his silver—and his wife's virginity. If anyone were to find out, this could do both Fiske's and her reputation great damage. He hadn't been able to look at her or talk to her all day and he had let the whole crew feel the force of his anger.

But in just a few words, she had humbled him. Made him feel like such a brute. Was she right? Was he no better than the Emperor, acting as if she was an object to be claimed? Had he let his anger and his own past hurt at being let down by those he loved prevent him from seeing what had really happened? The Emperor had taken her at will, against hers, and caused her trauma in the process. And Fiske had done the worst thing he could do and scolded her for it, when she had been brave and opened up to him.

He turned and his arms came round her, pulling her into his chest. 'Shhh,' he said, stroking her back, smoothing his hands over her hair. 'It's all right, Kassia.'

'It isn't. I never asked for any of this,' she said, resting her head against his shoulder. 'I never asked to be in his bride show, or for him to do the things he did. And I never asked for you to come along and ask me to marry you. I never thought I could be with a man physically again, after the things he did. But you… You made me want to try.'

Her words were like cold water on a fire.

'I see what kind of man you are, Fiske,' she said, pulling away from him slightly, to look up at him. 'But do you think me *liking* you makes me any less afraid? It doesn't. It only makes me more so, because of what that means—what could happen between us.'

She placed her hand over his chest. It was one of the first times she'd touched him of her own accord and he wondered if she could feel his heart pounding beneath her fingertips. 'He may have taken my body, but isn't my mind, my heart—the things I want to give freely— more important?'

Was she saying she thought one day she might be willing to give it all to him?

She looked in earnest—the way she had the night they'd met. And now he knew the full story, he ran over the events of the past few days again. Her crazy idea to run away. Her evident relief that Constantine hadn't picked her to be his bride and yet she'd still wanted to get away. It all made sense now. Even the way she flinched at his touch, though he'd been so sure their desire was mutual. She was frightened. And he had been a fool and rushed her.

Kassia's only fault had been not telling him sooner. And how could he scold her for withholding the truth, when he was keeping secrets of his own from her? Soon they'd be back at his settlement and she'd discover the truth about who he really was. And she wouldn't like it. After demanding nothing but honesty from her, what would she say?

It would be winter in Denmark now. Men would be returning from their raids in the west in time for the harvest. He wondered how the people would feel about his homecoming. Would he be able to command their respect? He now had the silver necessary to build up more support. And he'd proven he could lead and command an army. Hopefully stories of his feats in the Great City would have reached Danish shores ahead of his arrival.

Things would be different when he returned. Especially now he was married. And he hoped his people would like his wife. His men seemed to. As did he.

His eyes softened and he reached out to stroke her cheek. She looked exhausted, her lips taut, yet she was still achingly beautiful. 'I'm not angry with you—only with him and your parents for what they did. They took advantage of you and the situation. He abused his power. He is at fault here, Kassia, not you.' He pulled her back into his arms and she almost sagged against him in relief.

He felt angry at himself for ignoring her all day, like a petulant child, making her and himself feel worse, making her feel she was alone. He wanted to lower his head and kiss her again, to pick up where they left off last night, but he wasn't going to do anything unless she asked him to. He knew now he had to take this slow. He knew he had to help her…

Kassia was awoken by Fiske tugging on her shoulder. 'Kassia.'

She gasped, sitting bolt upright. She was shocked he was in here, at her side.

After they had made up last night, he had taken her to her tent and said goodnight at the door. She had been shocked to discover she was disappointed, wanting him to come inside and talk, maybe even hold her and give her the comfort she craved. But despite telling her he wasn't angry with her, he had kissed her on the forehead and told her to get some rest.

Seeing him here now, she felt a sliver of hope creep through her.

'Get up. You need to come with me,' he whispered.

'Where are we going?'

She cast off the furs and rubbed the sleep out of her eyes.

'Put these on and meet me outside,' he said, passing her a plain tunic and some woollen breeches.

She gave him a look. They weren't very attractive. Not like her usual exotic dresses made of silk in bright colours. But she imagined she would have to get used to plainer things when she was in Denmark.

'Don't even think about arguing. Where we're going, you don't want to stand out.'

Were they his clean clothes? She lifted the material to her nose and breathed in his familiar spicy scent.

Leaving the tent moments later, she felt ridiculous in the huge clothes that swamped her. Fiske looked up from where he was sitting waiting, on a rock, and grinned.

'I look awful!' She blushed, lifting up her arms and dropping them back down by her sides.

He grinned, coming towards her. 'Arms up,' he said and she rolled her eyes and obliged. But not before she removed the dagger he'd given her on the boat the night they'd first met out of her belt.

He raised his eyebrows, but he didn't take it off her.

'You don't mind?' she asked.

'Why would I? I did give it to you for your own protection.'

He fastened the belt tighter around her waist, before rolling up the sleeves. Goose bumps erupted over her arms where he touched her, and she shivered. She was so aware of him.

'Breathe, Kassia,' he whispered.

She was relieved when he stood back to admire his work. 'That's better. Although to be honest, you'd look good in anything. Come on.'

They set off down the path and she glanced back at the men, packing up the camp.

'What about the others?'

'We're going to meet back up with them later.'

'Where are we going?' She halted on the path. He was unnerving her, avoiding answering her questions. 'I'm not going any further until you tell me what's going on. You said we should stick together. You said we were heading for the river.'

He stopped, too, a little further down the track, looking back at her. 'And you said you trusted me.'

She swallowed.

'Do you?'

'I want to.' But trusting people meant getting hurt…

'We're heading to a market in a village not far from

here. I need some supplies before we continue with our journey. I didn't want to leave you alone with my men.'

'You don't trust *them*?'

'With my life. I just thought you'd be more comfortable with me. But if you'd rather stay...'

'No. You were right. I want to come. It's just my feet are in agony. I've never done so much walking.'

He gestured with his head to the path. 'Let's set off, then. The sooner we get back, the sooner we can get to the boat.' And they began to make their way over rocky terrain.

'Are all your men from Denmark, too?'

'Yes, they left with me to come here. Some have wives and children waiting for them at home, so are eager to get back.'

'And they left them to fight for you? For five years?'

'It was their choice. I didn't make them. But like me, they are all keen to start living for their own cause, rather than someone else's.'

'Were they seeking fame and fortune, too?'

'Just the glory,' he said. 'But I'm determined to reward them for their loyalty just as soon as I can.'

It was a rocky descent, Fiske climbing over one boulder, then waiting to help her, and she kept having to take his hand and accept his assistance. After a while, he kept hold of her hand, rather than letting her go each time, and she didn't mind. It felt good to be held.

She was glad he was more talkative this morning, asking her questions about her family, as if trying to get to know her better, and she him. She told him a little about her brother, and her horse-riding back in Constantinople. Her parents had never allowed her to do so, but she had been so incensed, eventually her brother had said he'd teach her in secret. And she'd loved their rides together. She missed him now he was gone.

The journey to the village passed quickly in Fiske's company and, approaching the bustle of the small market, Kassia saw it was nothing like the grand bazaars in Constantinople. Even so, the people and their wares enthralled her as they made their way through the tables laden with food, woodwork and wax goods, and alongside pens full of animals.

They passed a stall full of leather and Fiske halted. 'Would they fit you?' He nodded, gesturing to a pair of little boots. 'They might save your feet.'

He made her try them on and, once he'd laced her into them, he handed over a few coins to the vendor. She was touched and her feet were grateful.

'Now stay close,' Fiske whispered, tugging her behind him. 'Keep up.'

Fiske seemed to know where he was heading, striding out with purpose through the crowd, and she was surprised when they approached a stall with a woman selling tinctures and herbs. He spoke to her in the Danish tongue and Kassia didn't understand what they were saying, but she watched in fascination as the woman boiled up a concoction of herbs, then skimmed off the top of the mixture and handed it to him in a jar.

He paid for it with one of his metal armbands and they left.

'Come, let's go and sit over there,' he said, motioning to a grassy verge under the shelter of some trees.

She was loath to let go of his hand as they lowered themselves on to the ground, but he began rummaging around in his satchel for something. Finally, he retrieved an animal horn and poured the murky jar of liquid into it, before passing it to her.

'What is it?' she asked, sniffing the contents.

'It's a tea. You drink it.'

She turned up her nose. It didn't smell very good. 'Where's yours?'

He shook his head slightly. 'It's a special tea. Just for you.'

Her brow furrowed. 'What for?'

A muscle flickered in his jaw. 'It's pennyroyal. Juniper. Rosemary.' He ran his hand over his chin. 'When taken in large amounts, it can rid your body of an unwanted child...'

She reeled, her throat closing in shock. So that's why they were here. That's why they had left the others and made this journey alone.

'You have to understand... No man wants to take on the responsibility of another man's child! No man wants to spend their life wondering if they are the father. I can't be in any doubt... Honour is the most important thing to our people. My lineage is imperative to me.'

She nodded, mute, and he continued.

'What's worse... If you are with child and you have it, if the Emperor finds out that child is his heir, there's no telling what he might do.'

She gripped the horn tight. There was a compelling truth to what he was saying—she would be putting Fiske and everyone at risk if she bore the Emperor's child. They would never be safe. And she would never be rid of her memories. Her stomach churned. The thought of having the Emperor's child repulsed her.

She could tell Fiske thought he was helping her. Helping *them*. And she knew she had to do this, to prove her loyalty to him. Yet, staring down into the liquid, she felt disturbed. Uncertain. Fiske had sprung this upon her and she hadn't had time to think about it. He was asking her to drink the concoction without giving it any thought and, once again, she felt as if her will wasn't her own. That someone was making choices for her.

'Is it dangerous?' she asked, troubled.

'There may be some discomfort, but the healer promised it will bring no harm to you.'

'Just the baby. If there is one,' she clarified, wrapping her hand tighter around the ivory.

He nodded.

'What about in the future? If I wanted a family…?'

'Do you?' he asked.

'Yes, one day… Do you?'

'Yes. She said there would be no complications.'

Kassia nodded. 'Will I be judged by God?'

'I don't know… I don't believe in your one God, but many…'

She swirled the herbs around in the horn. What choice did she have? If she wanted any kind of future

with him, she had to drink this. She tentatively lifted
the cup up to her lips.

'What is it you say in Denmark?' she asked, trying
to make light of the situation. *'Skol?'* And she parted
her lips and tipped the vessel and its potent contents up
towards her mouth—but suddenly he slapped the horn
away, spilling the tonic down her tunic and on to the
grass.

'What the—?' she gasped.

He growled, getting to his feet, seemingly frustrated
with himself. He paced, his hands on his hips. 'Were
you really going to drink it?'

'Yes,' she said, frowning. 'Why? Was this some kind
of test?'

'Why would you do that? Why would you take it?'

'Because you asked me to,' she said, exasperated.
'And you're right. I don't want to be reminded of what
he did to me. I don't want his child.'

He raked his hand through his hair, letting out a long
breath. 'Unfortunately, I don't think that's our choice
to make now. We will have to leave it to the will of
the gods. I can't let you do it.' He came down on his
haunches and looked into her eyes. 'I'm sorry. I should
never have brought you here. Forgive me.' He stroked
his knuckles down her cheek. 'Let's try to forget about
it. For now.'

'But… What does that mean—for us?'

'I don't know…' he said, shaking his head. He stood,
holding out his hand for her to take, to help her up. 'Let's
just get through this journey to Denmark, all right? Let's

wait and see what happens. Let's wait for the gods to decide.'

She nodded, placing her hand in his, feeling an enormous lump in her throat she couldn't swallow down.

Chapter Five

By mid-afternoon they heard the sound of tumbling water again so he knew they were on the right track, getting closer and closer to the river. They were hoping to meet up with his men at a location past the rapids, where they could put the boat back in the water.

'We're almost there,' Fiske announced. He would be able to breathe a bit easier then. He would be back in his domain and there would be less chance of an ambush from the nomadic people once they were on the water.

But knowing they were nearly there didn't lift his mood. Fiske was feeling rotten. He couldn't believe he'd made her walk all the way to the market and back. The journey had been tough and he could see that she was tiring—yet not once did she grumble. She was made of strong stuff.

Still, he couldn't believe he'd put her through it—and for what? At the last moment he'd had second thoughts, decided he couldn't live with himself if he let her drink it. She might never forgive him for it and he didn't want to take the risk of causing her any harm, no matter what the healer had said. So he'd spilled the liquid.

But at least now he knew she'd been willing to do it for him, that whatever the outcome, she didn't want the Emperor's child. He should have perhaps explained he couldn't have any questions about his paternity, not given his position. But he could never seem to find the right words. It never seemed to be the right moment.

He had always prided himself on never feeling fear, yet the closer he was getting to his goal, the bigger the feeling of apprehension grew. He wasn't starting to have doubts about claiming back his title and his lineage. He knew another great battle lay ahead of him if he was to pursue what he wanted. More blood would be spilled. Blood that would be on his hands. And the responsibility of what was involved if he defeated his uncle would be great.

What if he didn't live up to expectations? What if he let his family and his people down, as many felt his father had? It would be so much easier to live a quiet, simple life—one like his new wife wanted. But could he put his lifelong ambitions aside?

He saw a deer dart through the trees up ahead. All of a sudden the animal slumped, and the hairs on the back of his neck stood on end. He had always had a strong awareness of his surroundings, honed from years of fighting, and he knew, instantly, that this was bad.

Fiske stopped dead and Kassia collided into his back.

'Sorry,' she gasped.

'Quiet,' he whispered, raising his fingers to his lips.

'Keep low,' he said, tugging her down into the undergrowth.

Apprehension twisted in his stomach and he reached for the hilt of his sword.

The thundering of horses' hooves sent his anxiety soaring and he unsheathed his sword. But it was too late. They were surrounded by dark-eyed, dark-haired men, with long moustaches, sat astride wild horses, the animals' nostrils flaring.

Fiske cursed, assessing the six men. Pechenegs.

No! He couldn't believe this was happening now. Not when they were so close to the river. It was all his fault, for breaking away from his men. He'd put Kassia in danger.

'Stay back. Stay behind me,' he whispered to her.

'Silver,' one of the men shouted and he could tell they didn't speak his language.

He lifted up his free arm. 'As you can see, I have none.'

'Our lands...' the leader gestured all around them '...you pass through. You pay with silver.'

Fiske shook his head. 'I have nothing.'

'Then you pay with woman.' The man grinned and his comrades all laughed.

Kassia's eyes swung to his. And the shaft of fury that charged through his body was intense. Why did other men think they could lay their hands on her? She belonged to him. She was his to protect. And no man would get near her, not on his watch.

'No.'

'Then you die anyway.'

He turned to Kassia, pulling her up close against his chest to whisper in her ear, 'When I say jump, you jump, all right?'

Her eyes widened. 'What?'

The men descended from their horses and he took his chance. He grabbed her upper arm and with all the strength he possessed, he yelled at her to jump and flung her over the cliff face. She screamed, but quickly thudded to the ground, landing on a ridge below.

His eyes found hers across the crevice and he nodded to her as she dusted herself down and stood, before he turned and charged towards the men, wielding his sword.

The Pechenegs attacked, but he was a far superior swordsman. He was a ruthless force, his power and prowess unwavering as he dynamically fought off one man, then another. Individually, these nomad barbarians were no match for him, but together, they lunged, crowding him.

He disposed of two of the men quickly, but he had to swing his sword wildly, fending off their thrusting blades as the others circled him.

His heart was in his mouth when he saw one of the men break away, heading towards the crevice, trying to get down to where Kassia was. She pressed her back against the rock face, trying to keep away from him on the narrow ledge.

Fiske knew he needed to get to her, to help her, but right now he was surrounded. His blows became more savage and brutal, injuring each of his enemies in turn, while trying to hold off their own viciously slicing blades, aware his face and clothes were covered in blood, unsure if it was his own or theirs. Sinking to his knees, he kept going, three against one. But he couldn't die here. He wasn't ready to go to Odin's Great Hall of Valhalla yet. Not before he'd avenged his father's death. Not before he'd returned home and claimed his family seat. And not before he'd made love to his beautiful wife…

Out of the corner of his eye he saw the man reach the rocky overhang above the ledge where Kassia was and he saw her remove the dagger from her belt. As the man dropped down, she held the knife to his throat.

'Don't move,' she said.

But the man barely missed a beat. He pushed her, shoving her body against the cliff face. She hit her head on a rock, making her wince, and the man saw his chance and launched for her, smacking her across the jaw. A tussle ensued and Fiske could barely concentrate on his own opponents, so desperate was his need to get to her. But she was putting up fierce resistance, fighting at his side, and he couldn't believe it. Had she been taught swordsmanship? The man's body suddenly slumped and hers sagged in relief. He couldn't believe it. Had she disposed of him?

He fought more ferociously, wanting this to be over, wanting to get to her, slashing and stabbing, until he was down to just one man, and he ran his sword through the brute's chest in a final, devastating blow.

He gave himself a moment. His body was burning, but he wasn't sure where he was hurt—he was drenched in blood, his own pumping through him. He was reluctant to turn and look at her, afraid of what he'd see in her eyes. Would she think him a monster?

He lifted the bottom of his tunic and wiped the material over his face, then slowly rose to his feet to make his way over to the bank. He reached out his arm for her to take. Her eyes were wide with shock.

'Come on, I've got you. Take my hand.'

She stepped on the body to get her higher and gripped his fingers, and he hoisted her up on to the grassy mound. She threw her arms around his neck, taking him by surprise.

'Are you hurt?' she gasped.

He held her arms, pulling her away from his bloodied body. 'It's nothing that won't heal. I'm more concerned about you.'

His hand came up to touch her jaw where the man had hit her and he checked over her face, her head where she'd hit the rock. She was bleeding.

'I'm fine,' she said.

'You were an asset, Kassia,' he said in admiration. 'I didn't know you knew how to fight.'

'My brother showed me a few tricks. I had planned to display them as my talent in the bride show, if the Emperor asked. I had visions of showing him what I could do with the blade you gave me.'

Fiske grinned. 'I would have liked to have seen his face if you'd done that.'

She bit her lip. 'I've never killed a man before,' she whispered, shaking her head in disbelief.

'You had no choice,' he said. He knew how hard it was to comprehend. He had been responsible for deciding if many should live or die. It was difficult to live with.

'You…you were…' she whispered.

'I didn't want you to see me like this,' he said, cutting her off, not wanting to hear her words.

'Why not? Isn't that who you are? A renowned warrior?'

'I'm not the barbarian people think I am.'

'I know that. I've truly never seen such strength and ferocity. You were incredible.'

He raised his head at her words of approval.

'Where did you learn to fight like that?' she asked.

'Where I come from, it is a way of life. Boys grow up learning to fight. It's how we're taught to defend our honour. It's how we can fulfil our destiny and die valiantly and go to Odin's Great Hall in Valhalla.'

'You wish for your life to be over?'

Her face was so close, he wanted to kiss her. He wanted to pull her close and hold her. But his body was still shaking from the fight, his skin covered in sweat and blood. 'No, not yet. There are still many things I want to do before I die. Things with you,' he said, leaning in closer, tucking her loose strands of hair behind her ear. 'When you're ready.'

She smiled.

'But right now, I think I need to have a wash.'

'There was a waterfall back there. Can you walk?'

He nodded, grimacing. 'It's my arm that's smarting. I'll get a better look when I get this blood off.'

She tucked her hand into his and they walked back along the path they'd trodden not long before, pleased to be getting away from the scattered bodies of the life-less men.

'Do you think there will be more of them coming?' she asked.

'I doubt it. They tend to move around in packs. Live out of wagons. We should be safe for now.'

Approaching the rushing cascade of water tumbling from the rocks above, she watched as Fiske unhooked his sword and belt and cast them down on to a rock. 'Do you want to go first?'

She shook her head fiercely. 'We should see how bad your injuries are.'

'You might need to help me with this,' he said, try-ing to tug his tunic up over his chest.

She gulped, but it was no time to be shy. He was hurt and he needed her assistance. She curled her fingers around the bottom of the material and deftly lifted it up and over his chest and his arms, trying not to hurt him—and she stifled a gasp when his bloodied but magnificent chest came into view.

'You are hurt!' she cried, instantly worried at the sight of his wounds.

'It looks worse than it is.'

And then she saw dark, snake-like ink wrapped around his muscled arms, winding its way across his chest, and she was momentarily distracted. Up through the middle, carved across his chest, was what looked like a giant spear. She had never seen anything like it before. Only on rune stones or carvings—never on someone's body. It was intricate. Fascinating. It made her want to run her fingers over it, explore it, and she caught herself.

He put his hands to the waistband of his breeches. 'I can do the rest. You might want to turn around.'

Seeing he was about to strip off completely, she inhaled sharply and spun around. She lowered herself down on the rock next to his discarded tunic, facing away from him. She heard the soft thud of his clothes and then his legs wading through the shallow pool to the cold, cascading water.

Sitting there waiting, the temptation was too great and she glanced over her shoulder. His back was turned towards her, so she allowed her eyes to stealthily roam over his massive, muscular body and down. They widened in wonder at the curve of his buttocks. He was… perfect. The ink covered his back, too, strange symbols carved into his flesh, which moved as he raised his arms to wash himself. And she suddenly realised what she was doing. She didn't want to be caught staring! She spun back round, feeling a blush spread across her chest and her cheeks.

'What is all that? On your body. What does it all mean?' she called out to him, raising her voice to be heard over the roaring water, fiddling with a mark on her breeches.

There was a pause before she heard his voice behind her, closer than she'd expected, and she could tell he was moving towards her. She swallowed. If she turned round now… She heard him pick up his breeches and listened to him tugging them back on.

'I'm decent.'

She turned round slowly, trying to prepare herself for the sight of him. Clean again, his chest was impressive. Beautiful. Her mouth dried.

He pointed to the snake-like creature, covered in scales, eating its own tail. 'It's a bit of a family crest— my father had someone do it. It's meant to represent the cycle of life. But my father also told me it was a way of remembering I should rely only on myself.'

'Is that what you believe?' She frowned.

'No. I don't think he was right all of the time. I trust my men with my life,' he said, running the inside of his tunic over the droplets of water on his arms, then his hair.

Jealousy smarted. She wanted him to feel that way about her—that he could trust her. Rely on her. Would he ever, after their rocky start? She wanted him to know that she wouldn't let him down. Because that was how she was starting to feel about him after he'd protected her since the beginning, from that first night on the boat. Now he had saved her life again.

'And the other? What is that?' she asked, pointing to the giant spear.

'Gungnir—it's Odin's spear. It represents authority. It's also meant to bring protection.'

The spear was sliced in half with a nasty gash and, courageously, she reached out to press her hand against his chest with her fingertips. His skin was cool to the touch, but she could feel the warmth of his blood beneath and the steady beat of his heart. She was finding she wanted to touch him, when she'd never wanted to get close to a man before.

'Are you in pain?' she asked. 'It looks nasty.'

'They're clean at least. More scars to look forward to...'

'What are those markings on your back?' And too late, she realised what she'd said.

His eyes narrowed on her. 'How do you know about those?'

Her cheeks burned at being caught out and he tried, badly, to stifle a smile. 'They're runes. They spell out Courage, Honour and Determination.' He put a foot up on the rock next to her and leaned down close. 'I thought you weren't going to peek. Did you like what you saw, Kassia?'

'I—I was merely checking if you had any wounds.'

He grinned wider. 'And do I?'

'You might have an extra one in a moment!'

He laughed freely then and she couldn't help but smile, too.

'That gash on your arm is the deepest. Maybe we could wrap something around it?' she said, fighting for composure.

He nodded, ripped off some material from the bottom of his tunic with his teeth and passed it to her.

'Would you mind?'

She took it and held his upper arm—his skin warm and solid beneath her touch—as she began to wrap the material around him, aware she was holding her breath, careful with her movements so she didn't cause him any more pain. Not that he seemed to be bothered by it.

When she was finished, he inspected it, before taking her chin in his hand. 'Thank you,' he said, before grinning at her again. 'And just so you know, you can examine me whenever you want. You just tell me when you want to get a closer look, all right?'

She went to swat him across the other arm and he attempted to duck out of the way, then he was pulling on his tunic, covering himself up, and she felt the faint wash of disappointment. She thought she could stare at his body all day.

'If you want to wash, too, I promise *I* won't peek.'

She nodded, standing up. 'Will you teach me about your beliefs, when we get to Denmark?' she asked. 'I'd like to better understand them.' Perhaps then she could better understand him, she thought.

'I'd like that. But I don't think we'll be getting any closer to home today. The light's fading fast. Shall we camp here tonight and leave at first light to catch up with the others? To be honest, I think we could both do with the rest. That cave over there will make a pretty good shelter.'

'All right,' she said, biting her lip. Could she really be alone with him all night? She knew now he would be true to his word and not touch her, but she was starting to wonder if she would be able to bear it. What if she wanted him to? 'Will the men wait for us?'

'Of course. I'll go and light a fire while you wash,' he said. 'I'll be within hearing distance if there's any problems.'

She nodded and watched him retreat. When he was out of sight, she stripped off quickly and braced herself for the shock of the cold water. It was freezing, but it felt good to wash off the dirt and grime of the past few days. She ran her hands over her body, splashing water over her face, under her arms and between her legs, and suddenly she wondered what it would feel like to have him touch her there. She had never wanted a man to touch her before. But Fiske…

By the time she'd dried off and pulled the oversized clothes back on, he'd lit a fire in the small entrance to the rock face and had laid out the furs they had between them for her to sit on.

'Better?' he asked, taking in her wet hair.

'Much.'

'You're getting quite the bruise on your forehead.'

She lifted her fingers to touch the bump and winced. 'Is this a good idea, to light a fire?'

'It'll be well hidden in this cave. And I don't want you freezing to death. Are you hungry?'

She nodded.

'Those men killed a deer earlier. I'm going to go and see if I can retrieve it.'

She shook her head and reached out to touch his arm. 'No, don't go.'

He considered her for a moment. 'Go together?'

She nodded.

For the first time, it felt as though they were working as a team and it felt good. Returning to the spot on the cliff where the fight had taken place, Kassia shuddered. They found the deer a short way into the forest, an arrow to its neck. 'The poor thing,' Kassia said, crouching down beside it.

'This deer saved your life,' Fiske said. 'If it wasn't for him, I wouldn't have known those men were upon us.'

She paled.

'When I saw them approach, I thought that was it. I should have warned you how dangerous this is. I'm sure part of you is regretting coming with me.' He grimaced.

Did he mean here, to retrieve the animal, or with him on this journey to Denmark? She shook her head. She didn't regret either, despite all that had come to pass so far. With him, she felt more alive than ever.

Still, she was glad when they made it back to the safety of the cave and he set to cooking a little of the meat. She was starving. She watched him stoke the fire, the flames lighting up his face, flickering in his eyes.

'We do a lot of this—sitting around fires, telling stories and singing—back at home in Denmark. I'm afraid it won't be quite what you're used to. There will be no grand carnivals or chariot races for entertainment.'

'What? No auctioning of women?' she said wryly.

He shook his head. 'None of that either.'

'I won't miss any of those events.' She shrugged. 'I never enjoyed them much before.'

'No? What did you do for enjoyment?'

'Well, riding, obviously. And I liked to read. To learn.'

'I didn't know women were given an education.'

'Those who are more fortunate were allowed more freedom, although it was limited. But my father did at least allow me to study. I liked music, mathematics, astronomy…'

'You like the stars?' he asked, surprised, handing her a few pieces of meat off the tip of his blade.

'Doesn't everyone?' She looked up now and could see hundreds glittering down on them in the clear night sky. 'What do the women do in Denmark?' she asked, before taking a bite. It tasted delicious.

'There is always much work to do on the land, or with the animals, or the children. Women cook, but they also fight. In Denmark, you can be a shield maiden if you want to.'

'A shield maiden? You mean a fighter? Do such women exist? People have always made me feel my only worth is in my looks. I wish to be respected for more than that. My work or skills…'

'Let's be clear. I'm not advising you to fight. I would not want you getting hurt. I'm just saying perhaps in Denmark you can be who you want to be,' he said, repeating his words from the first night she met him. It amazed her that he was bringing it up again now, as if her needs were important. 'If you decide to stay.'

He ate a few morsels of meat himself and she was glad to see him eat. He needed to keep up his strength.

'Is that not strange, that you had to leave there and come to Constantinople, looking for what you needed, whereas I had to leave the city to do the same?'

He stared at her over the flames. 'I found what I wanted. I hope you find what you're looking for, too.'

He stoked the fire again, the heat reaching up, wrapping around them. 'Why don't you get some sleep now, Kassia? I'll keep guard for a while.'

'You need to rest more than I.'

He rolled his eyes. 'Are you going to argue with me again?'

She raised her hands in defeat. 'All right, I'll go.'

Kassia sighed and made her way inside the cave, and curled up on her side on the furs, facing away from him into the darkness of the cave. She could hear him sharpening his sword, as she'd noticed he always did at night, and there was something reassuring about it. He'd told her he didn't think they'd be attacked again—not tonight—but if they were, she knew he'd be ready.

She had never seen anyone fight as he had out there. His strokes had been masterful, demonstrating why he had become the leader in Constantinople—why the Emperor had chosen him. Why his men followed him. She had seen first hand why he had earned his reputation. His blows were controlled but lethal.

She had been afraid when that man had approached her on the ledge, but her eyes had sought out Fiske's and she'd drawn from his strength and fought back. Why was it that men thought they could take what they wanted from her? And how ironic was it that the man she now wanted to touch her wasn't trying to get her to lie with him at all? He was keeping his distance, telling her to go to sleep. Had he given up?

She was in awe of him. And his body… He was a man of many contradictions, she thought. He had a fearsome exterior. He was the largest, strongest man she'd ever encountered. But he was soft on the inside. No, not soft, but kind. That's why she felt safe with him.

He had shown such careful restraint with her, never forcing her to do anything she didn't want to do. In fact, since this morning, he had barely touched her at all and she was disturbed to find she was finding it infuriating. She checked herself—did she want him to touch her?

She thought about the kiss they'd shared the other night—the feel of his mouth on hers—and she turned over, flipping on to her back. He said he was never going to touch her again—did he mean it? When she had thrown her arms around him earlier, he had removed them from around his neck.

The thought of him never touching her, or kissing her again, left her feeling bereft, frustrated—especially when they were in such close proximity. It was making her want things she had never wanted before. And she knew, after fleeing from his arms the other night, she would probably need to be the one to broach it…

Lying near to him, in this small space, listening to his movements, his breathing, she wasn't sure she'd ever be able to get to sleep like this. She was all too aware of him. Her thoughts drifted to where he would make her sleep back at his home. Would she be expected to share his bed? Surely it would bring shame upon him if he brought a wife home and they slept apart? She felt guilty that she'd spent the night before alone in the tent. What had his men thought? Fiske had put her feelings before his pride and reputation, she realised.

She turned to look at his profile in the darkness, sat with his back against the wall, his legs outstretched. He was a good man. He had kept his word and hadn't done anything she hadn't wanted him to do, despite telling her of his desire. And yet he didn't seem to be suffering now, like she was.

Suddenly, he put down his blade and got to his feet, leaving the cave.

She sat up. Had he heard or seen something?

Frustratedly throwing off the furs, she followed him out. 'What is it?' she said, startling him. 'Where are you going?'

He spun round to look at her and raked a hand through his hair. He looked haunted.

'What are you doing out here, Kassia? Go back to bed!' he said in his deep, cool voice.

'I can't sleep.'

He grimaced. 'If I knew the cure for that, I wouldn't be wandering around out here myself.'

'I'm worried about you. You need to rest your wounds.'

'To be honest, rest is the last thing on my mind right now. I can't stay in there, Kassia, sitting beside you…' He looked tortured. 'I want you too much.'

She felt a coil of cautious hope unfurl in her stomach at hearing his words.

'But I know I told you I wouldn't touch you again.' He tried to smile, but the corners of his mouth collapsed. 'And I don't want to break my promise.'

She took a step towards him and took his hand in hers. She knew she had to be brave. She knew she had to fight for what she wanted. For both of them. She raised his hand to her lips and kissed the top of it. 'What if I said I wanted you to?'

His brow furrowed. 'Do you?'

'Yes. But I'm still afraid. Not of you, just…'

'I'm not going to hurt you.'

'I know that,' she said, lowering their entwined hands, stepping closer towards him.

'You want me?' he asked again, as if he didn't quite believe it. 'I want you to be sure.'

'Yes. I just…don't know if I can do this,' she said and felt her legs tremble.

'I understand. Why don't we just sit for a while? We don't have to do anything,' he said, tucking her hair behind her ear. 'I just want to hold you. That will be enough.' He pulled her close, tugging her into his arms, and kissed her forehead softly.

'I can do that.'

He took her hand and led her back into the cave. He sat down on the furs, his back against the wall, and wrapped an arm around her, pulling her head into the curve of his body, holding her close.

Her breathing was erratic as she curled into him, her hand coming up to rest on his solid chest, her knees tucked up against his thighs. It felt comforting, exciting, his large hand stroking her arm, causing her to shiver. She nuzzled in closer, between his shoulder and his neck, breathing in the warm, spicy scent of him.

'You smell of mimosa and fig trees,' he said, breathing in her hair. 'How can that be?'

She smiled. 'My father had fig trees back at home.'

'Will you miss it there?'

'No,' she said honestly. 'I don't think I will.'

Her fingertips courageously stole beneath the opening of his tunic, circling over his skin and the ink that fascinated her, but his hand came up to cover hers, as if to stop her.

'Am I hurting your wounds?' she asked, her voice throaty.

'No. It's just your touch is like flames dancing across my skin, stoking my desire. I'm a patient man, but even my restraint has limits… I thought we were just going to sit. Talk.'

She liked the thought of her touch sending him into a frenzy and, wanting to torture him a little bit more, she bravely pressed her lips against the column of his throat. He groaned and pulled away, to look into her eyes.

'Kassia…'

He had crystal-clear eyes and a beautiful mouth. Generous, just like his heart. 'I want you to kiss me again. Please, Fiske…'

Answering her wishes, he brought his hands up to hold her face and lowered his head to plant a soft, chaste kiss against her lips. But it wasn't enough. She knew he was trying to take it slow—for her—but she wanted more. She wanted him to put his tongue inside her mouth again.

She brought her hands up to hold his jaw, drawing him closer, and finally he parted his lips, his tongue seeking out hers, giving in to what she wanted and stroking deeply inside her mouth. She gasped at the heated feelings flickering south inside her.

It was a sensual exploration and it was as if he wanted to leave no part of her mouth undiscovered. The kiss went on and on and she never wanted it to end.

At some point Fiske lowered himself to the ground

and dragged her with him, so they were lying side by side. He pulled her up against his body as he continued to kiss her, slowly, deeply, passionately, his hands tangling in her wet hair.

'Your hair feels like silk,' he whispered.

And she reciprocated, her palms smoothing over his chest and stealing over his broad shoulders, learning the lines of him, before threading up through his own hair, pulling it out of its band. She luxuriated in the feel of it—she had never known a man to have the same length hair as her before, and she wondered why he never wore it loose.

He rolled her over on to her back and pulled away slightly, hovering over her, to look down into her eyes. 'Is this all right?'

'Yes.' She nodded.

'If you want me to stop…'

'I don't,' she said, shaking her head.

She was grateful he was asking, that he was taking it slowly, trying to make sure she was ready. But she didn't want him to stop. Not now. She wanted to get closer to him.

Propped up on an elbow, he let his thumb smooth over her lips and along her jaw. His fingers trailed down her neck and she lifted her chin slightly as the tips grazed her collarbone and lower, running along the edge of her tunic. Her heart skittered.

'I'm happy just talking, if you'd rather…'

She shook her head. 'Don't stop.'

'I want to explore you everywhere. With my hands.

And my mouth. Are you sure you want me to continue?' he whispered.

She nodded, her heartbeat nearing hectic. She never knew she could feel like this. That a man's touch could feel so good. That he could make you *want* so much.

His hand moved down to flatten over one breast and her lips parted as he ran his thumb over the taut peak straining through the material. He continued to watch her face as he gently squeezed her flesh and her hands came up around his back, delving under his tunic to run her fingers over the scars and markings she knew lay beneath.

She had wanted to touch him since she'd seen him in the waterfall. Even before that. She was in awe of the sheer size and beauty of him. She bunched up the material and he lifted himself away from her so she could take it off. Suddenly it was gone and her fingers were free to roam over his broad expanse of solid, warm, golden skin.

Following her lead, he pulled at the ties at her neckline, loosening the material, and tugged the tunic out of her breeches, smoothing it up over her chest. But suddenly she froze, her hands coming up to cover her breasts.

He halted, staring down at her. 'That's not very fair,' he said, his lips curling upwards. 'You get to see and touch me and I don't you?'

She knew he was jesting and she smiled. It helped her to relax a little. 'I… No one's ever seen me without clothes on before. Except for my maid.'

He frowned. 'What about—?' And then he stopped.

He obviously thought better about bringing up the Emperor's name.

She shook her head. 'He did it from behind. He was in too much of a hurry.'

He swore again, and raked a hand over his hair. 'I'm sorry, Kassia. That's not what it's meant to be like. I hate that he did that to you. I can't bear to think about it.'

She nodded. 'Then don't,' she said, reaching for him again, planting a kiss against his lips.

'How old are you, Kassia?' he asked. 'I don't even know that simple fact about you. I barely know anything about the woman I married, yet I want to. I want to know everything.'

'I'm certainly someone I don't even recognise when I'm with you.'

'Is that a good thing?'

'Yes. I think so… I'm ten and eight winters. And you?'

'Six winters older.'

'And I'm guessing you've done this before. A lot?' she asked.

'Not a lot, no… I've spent most of my time fighting, remember?'

'There's no woman waiting for you back at home?'

'If there was, would I have agreed to marry you?' he said.

'What if I don't live up to them? Your other women.'

He looked incredulous. 'Kassia, you're the most beautiful woman I've ever seen. You can't disappoint me. You are the only woman I want to think about.'

Slowly, she lowered her hands and raised her body off the ground, holding her arms aloft, allowing him to pull the tunic free and lift it over her head and up her arms before discarding it. She shivered as the cool air hit her skin.

Laying her back down, he held her hands loosely above her head, as his gaze lowered to look at her, travelling over her rosy peaks and bronze skin, and her breath caught. Her stomach tightened.

His eyes darkened with a hunger she hadn't seen before—perhaps he'd been hiding it from her, worried it would scare her off. But now his gaze made her writhe restlessly, craving his touch.

'You are perfection,' he whispered and she whimpered.

His hands released hers to curve over her bare skin, trailing down her throat and her shoulders to cup her breasts, his thumbs stroking over her nipples. He kissed her again, his taut stomach pressing against her side, skin on skin, and she trembled at the connection.

'Still all right?' he asked, his voice raw and husky.

She nodded and he kissed her forehead. Somehow, it felt like real intimacy, that he truly cared, and she pulled his mouth back down on to hers, harder, deeper than before.

When he broke away, his lips followed the same heated path his fingers had moments before, leaving a trail of burning kisses down her neck and over the swells of her hot, thrusting breasts.

She gasped as his tongue curled around one rosy peak, sucking her into his mouth, making her arch her back off the ground, before he moved on to the other, lathering it in the same way, while his lower body pressed against hers. She could feel the hard ridge of him, the impact she was having on him, digging into her hip and she felt hot. Needy.

His kisses continued between her breasts and down, over her stomach, until he pulled away to sit up. His hands covered the buckle of her belt. 'Can I take this off?'

She nodded, chewing her lip, as he unfastened it and pulled the leather away from her skin, the oversized breeches almost falling away, before he deftly swept them down over her legs and pulled them off.

She pressed her knees together, trying to cover her exposed body with her hands, squirming beneath him, but he growled and gripped her wrists, fastening them either side of her.

'You are the most beautiful woman I've ever seen,' he whispered. 'I'm your husband. I'm allowed to look at you. If you don't want me to, maybe you're not ready. We could wait…'

They could, but his words just made her want him even more. Why couldn't she have met him before… before she'd been approached for the bride show? Before all of that had happened?

She let out a long, slow breath. She knew he was right. What was the point in trying to hide from him? If she wanted to be close to him, she needed to be brave. She told herself to relax and she lay back, offering herself up to him. He released her and as his heated gaze swept over her, taking in every inch of her, liquid heat pooled between her legs and she felt her legs part in restless anticipation.

She thought back to the public scrutiny at the bride show, but this was nothing like that. This was making her feel powerful, seeing the effect she was having on him. And she felt a hunger for him—a craving, like nothing she'd ever felt before.

'I told you I wouldn't touch you again unless you asked me to. Is this what you want?'

'Yes,' she groaned. 'Fiske, please.'

'All right, *kyria.*'

He stood and released his own belt, removing his breeches, and her eyes widened at the sight of him— he was huge! She bit her lip as he came back down and parted her ankles with his hands, kneeling between her legs. She gulped as his eyes glittered down at her in the fading firelight and instinct had her trying to squeeze her knees together, wanting to stop the ascent of his gaze and his touch.

'Kassia, relax,' he said, running his hands up her calves and over her knees, and back down again before roaming higher again, over her thighs. 'This is all about your pleasure. No pain. I promise.'

She couldn't believe it when she gave in and allowed him to push her knees apart, exposing herself to him. She covered her brow with her arm, helpless. He edged closer, until her bottom was raised off the ground and the back of her legs covered his thighs. She licked her lips, her mouth dry, unsure what he was going to do.

'I'm just going to touch you with my fingers. All right?'

His words made her body go up in flames. She felt flustered. Feverish.

His hands slid down unhurriedly over her thighs and when his thumbs met at the juncture of her legs, tangling between her dark mass of curls, she gasped. She kept her eyes on his as he parted her, stroking her gently, and her breath caught at the intimacy. It felt… oh! He was so gentle as he stroked her, his dark eyes watching her, and when his thumb edged inside her wet, silky opening, she cried out in shocked pleasure.

'Does that feel good, *kyria*?'

She raised herself up on her elbows, and further, wanting to get closer, and he pulled her up on to his lap, his hand still stroking her between them, and she clasped her fingers around his neck, holding on tight. He placed little kisses to her neck and shoulders while his finger circled her tiny blossoming bud, over and again, making her writhe wildly.

He uncurled one of her hands from around his neck and moved it down, wrapping her fingers around his hard shaft. 'I don't want you to be afraid of me,' he said, resting his forehead against hers, showing her how to move her hand up and down him.

'I'm not.'

As if he wanted to be sure, he pushed a long finger inside her and her head tipped forward, groaning in ecstasy, before he removed it to stroke her slick wetness again. She wrapped her body around his, tighter, and his tongue swept between her lips again. Slowly, his fingers roamed around to squeeze her soft, smooth bottom, kneading her sensitive flesh.

'Do you think you're ready?' he whispered.

Her heart began to pound and nerves fluttered low in her stomach. 'I don't know. I just know I want you so much, I want to try.'

'Tell me if you want to stop.'

He lifted her slightly, as if she were no weight at all, before gently lowering her down on to him. She felt him right there, at her entrance, nudging into her flesh, and she buried her head in his neck.

He pulled back.

'It might help if you look at me.'

Bracing her hands on his shoulders, she accepted just the silky tip of him, before her tight, tense muscles clenched around him and she halted.

'You're doing well. I'm in no hurry,' he whispered, kissing her neck, her cheeks. 'You feel so good, I never ever want this to end.'

He kissed her again and she sank a little lower, but he was so big, she didn't think she could take him in any further. Her eyes widened in appeal for assistance. 'Fiske…'

He lowered her down on to her back, coming over her body, holding himself up with his forearms. He stroked her hair away from her damp forehead.

'Is this all right?' His body was huge and she knew he didn't want to frighten her…but she loved his build. It didn't scare her. It was magnificent.

'Yes,' she choked, wrapping her legs around his back, wanting to give him better access, to please him, but still worried she couldn't. And she realised she was no longer frightened of doing this, she was just scared of disappointing him.

He stroked her face some more, kissing her slowly, before raising his head and smiling down at her, as if he was giving her time to get used to his initial invasion of her.

'You know I've wanted to do this from the moment I met you. I was tempted to do as you asked that night and take you away from there. You might have been trying to steal my boat, but I think you stole my affections instead.' He grinned.

And she smiled up at him. 'I can't think of another man who could have tempted me away across the sea, who I'd marry on a whim.' She smiled and felt herself relaxing beneath his thighs.

'Ready to try again?'

She nodded and, as he took her mouth with his lips again, he gave another thrust of his hips, breaching her further, nudging a little more inside. She'd barely had time to catch her breath before he penetrated her again, this time easing inside her all the way, and she gasped out her surprise and unexpected pleasure. 'Oh.' His movements were masterful, melting her insides, and she grappled wildly with his shoulders.

'You feel...incredible,' he whispered.

'So do you.'

Suddenly, her fear was gone and she felt hot. She just wanted...needed...more of him. Everything he could give. She wondered at her good fortune. Her father had tried to arrange a marriage for her, but she'd known her own heart.

He thrust again, harder this time, and she met him halfway, crying out at the exquisite sensations he was creating. She clung to his beautiful bottom, pulling him closer, and he gripped her knees, ruthlessly pushing them back against her shoulders, spreading her wider as he thrust again, taking her completely, as if he wanted to be part of her. As if he wanted to leave his mark, brand her as his own, wipe out all the bad memories and replace them with the good.

She was blinded with pleasure and didn't think there could be anything more intimate as he stared down into her eyes, surging torturously slowly, deeply, but relentlessly, slicked with sweat, unyielding, as if he would stop at nothing until he'd drawn every last drop of rapture from her body.

She began to thrash about, not sure how much more of this she could take, crying out in awe and wonderment, spluttering his name, warning him she was going crazy. As if he, too, had lost all restraint, he began to move quicker, frantic now, needing everything from her, and as she screamed in pleasure, her climax taking over her whole body, she felt his explosion deep inside her and knew his own release had been just as powerful as her own.

Chapter Six

Fiske lay on his side, curled around his wife's stunning body, feeling as if something profound had just happened. Their lovemaking had been remarkable, like nothing he'd ever felt before.

When he'd climaxed inside her, it had taken a while for his body to stop shuddering. He'd known he should roll off her, aware he was probably crushing her with his big body, but he didn't have the desire or inclination to move. He had never felt so sated. They had fitted perfectly together, and moved in unison, and the force of his release had been overwhelming. He hoped it had been just as good for her.

Needing to know if he had pleased her, he'd lifted his head to look down at her.

She'd brought her hand up to hold his jaw. She ran her thumb over the dent in his chin. 'Thank you. It was better than I ever thought it could be. Now I know what it's meant to be like…' She'd smiled up at him.

And his heart and his pride had swelled. It really had never been so good and he wondered at his good fortune. He couldn't sleep before, wondering what it would be like. Now he knew, why would he ever want to sleep again? And now he was wide awake, thinking that once they got back home, he would have her in his bed every night, that he could have her any time he wanted… It was as if all his dreams were coming true.

Yet things would be different when they reached Aarhus. He would have responsibilities again, and she would be one of them. He wondered how she'd be treated when they got there. Would she be seen as different from his people?

Her beauty would certainly make her stand out and many of his enemies would no doubt want to claim her for themselves. He would constantly be worried for her safety. She would be a distraction at a time when he needed to focus and when he had to leave, to go off and fight, he wouldn't want to… Right now, he didn't want to let her out of his arms, let alone his sight.

She was his perfect woman. From her silky black hair to her exotic eyes and burnished skin, her long legs that had wrapped around him and the way she'd felt as he'd surged inside her, thrusting deeper and deeper… He hoped he hadn't been too forceful. He hoped instead he'd managed to banish some of her darker memories, replacing them with good ones.

That was the only thing that was stopping him rolling her over on to her belly and thrusting into her once more, impaling her on the furs beneath him and doing it all over again, for he knew she would be sore this morning after his thorough taking of her. Given what she had said about the Emperor forcing her from behind, he thought better of it.

Part of him wanted to find his men, put the boat back in the water, and sail right back to Constantinople and teach the Emperor a lesson. How could Constantine have abused his power like that? And what kind of man did that make *him*? That he'd served someone like that for five winters… He determined if he was successful in his uprising against his uncle, if he should come to rule, he would use his power for good.

It was strange. He had longed to return to Denmark, eager to take back what was rightfully his, but the closer they got, the nearer Kassia was getting to finding out who he was and he felt awful for deceiving her. He was worried what her reaction would be when she found out. Would she still want him?

Kassia began to stir and she turned round and stretched in his arms, making him hard in an instant, and then she pressed her lips against his, adoration shining in her almost-black eyes, and he felt guilt slap him in the face.

She had made herself vulnerable to him, shared everything with him willingly, and he had lied to her about something so fundamental—himself. Who he was. His lineage. He wasn't the man she thought she'd made love to. And despite his desire to have her again, the thought had him pulling away, more forcefully than he meant to.

'We ought to be going,' he said, removing himself from her arms, his voice curt. 'The men will be waiting for us. I'd better get dressed. So had you.' And although it pained him, he disentangled himself from her body, leaving her lying there as he got up and stalked out of the cave.

When Kassia emerged a while later, fully clothed and ready to leave, he knew straight away that he'd hurt her. She was trying hard not to look at him, as if her invisible shield wall was up again. He cursed himself. Part of him wanted to pull her to him, tell her he was sorry and take her back inside the cave to make everything better. Yet there was a little voice inside his head telling him maybe this was for the best.

They'd both got what they wanted from each other for now. To take things any further, to get any closer, would be dangerous to his heart. Especially if he had to leave her when he got home. Especially if she was going to leave him when she discovered the truth.

'Ready to go?' he asked.

She nodded stiffly.

It took a while to traverse down the cliff to the river, climbing over rocks, scrambling through scree, and they both fell into silence. He was much more stable on the slippery terrain than she was and kept holding out his hand to help her, but she was careful not to touch him, refusing his assistance, as stubborn as ever.

Back on the path, with her walking ahead of him, he couldn't help but focus on her swaying bottom in those ridiculous breeches. Part of him wanted to tug her back, to kiss her and make her his again, as soon they would no longer be alone.

When they met up with his men again, he wouldn't be able to kiss her and touch her at will, and suddenly, he wished he'd taken her again this morning, when he'd had the chance, for now the rest of their journey stretched out before them. And yet he wasn't sure she'd want him again now. Her barrier was back up. *Helvete*, he was such a fool.

When they caught sight of the boat and his men, Fiske called out to them and they came charging over to greet them, genuine relief on their faces. He embraced his two best men, Arne and Erik, and they even gathered Kassia into a hug, pleased to see her, too, welcoming her into their fold.

He let out a breath he hadn't realised he'd been holding. They'd made it. She was safe.

'We were beginning to worry about you. At first we thought… Well, we thought you wanted to be alone.' Arne grinned, punching him on the shoulder and throwing Kassia a wink. 'But then we thought the worst. That maybe the Pechenegs…'

'They tried—and failed.'

'Very glad to hear that.'

But all of a sudden arrows flew through the air behind them, as a group of men let out a tribal, shrieking cry. Their horses began to charge down the steep hillside towards them, from the direction he and Kassia had just walked. They must have passed the waterfall and the open cliff, where their comrades' bodies still lay.

Fiske went cold all over. If they'd passed through just hours earlier… It didn't bear thinking about.

Arrows landed all around them, narrowly missing them, and Fiske grabbed Kassia's arm and flung her forward, racing towards the boat. He had never been so glad to see his father's ship.

They all piled in, using the oars to push themselves away from the bank as wooden darts landed in the hull around them. But within moments, they were a fair distance away, the men rowing with all their might, leaving the Pechenegs floundering on the side of the ravine, raising their weapons and shouting in their native tongue.

'Is anyone hurt?' Fiske asked, before turning to Kassia and taking her hand. 'Are you all right?'

She nodded, but removed herself from his grasp. His eyes narrowed on her.

'Please don't,' she warned him. 'Not in front of your men.'

He looked at her in disbelief, angry that she didn't want the others to see them touching. Cross that she was rejecting him again. But what did he expect, after his cool treatment of her this morning? And she was right—the men didn't need to watch them engage in any displays of affection, not when they were missing their own women.

She pulled away from him, putting distance between them, and he didn't like it, yet he knew it was his fault. He had created a gulf between them and he didn't like himself much for it.

She began to walk away from him.

'Where are you going?' he asked, incredulous.

'To sit over there. We don't need to be in each other's company all the time, do we?'

'I guess not,' he replied.

He raked a hand through his hair, trying to concentrate on the river and where they were heading. Maybe this was for the best. He had to keep his strength for the rest of the journey and focus on what was to come when they returned home. With her, he was at risk of forgetting everything else.

Kassia confined herself to the front bench of the boat, alone again.

She was still reeling from what had happened last night—and this morning. It had been the best night of her life. Fiske had made her feel whole again and she had thought herself in love. She had woken up happy for the first time in months, content in his arms, not needing anything else. Then she had leaned in to kiss him and he'd jerked away from her, getting to his feet so fast, it had startled her, making her wonder what she'd done wrong.

She was reeling with hurt and anger. How could he push her away, after the things they'd done just hours before? After he'd slept wrapped around her body all night? How could he pull away from her so easily, when she never wanted to let him go?

Standing in the cave on trembling legs, she'd hurriedly thrown on her clothes and tried to focus on packing up their things. She didn't want to seem as though she was sitting there pining for him, waiting for him to come back and make love to her all over again.

And then it struck her. He'd claimed his wife—he'd got what he wanted. Was he now sated? Did he not want it to happen again? Did he regret what they'd done?

Thinking about it now, he hadn't whispered any words of love… He had stripped her bare last night— her body and her emotions—and now she felt exposed. She had almost told him she was falling in love with him. But for him, had it just been sex? Sex with his wife which was his due. It was just something men and women, husbands and wives, did together. He might have taken care of her body, but it didn't mean he cared for her.

Vulnerability and confusion washed through her, but she knew she had to guard herself, to protect her heart from getting even more damaged. And most of all, she was determined to keep her pride.

Glancing around the men, she felt different and she wondered if everyone else could tell—if everyone was aware of what they'd done together. Or did it just feel like this great big, enormous thing to her?

Seeing Arne holding his arm, she moved over to him, concerned. 'Are you hurt?'

'It's just a scratch.'

'Do you all say that when you've been injured?' she asked wryly. 'I may not be able to help row the boat yet, but I do know how to patch up a wound if you'd like me to.'

He nodded and released his hand from his arm. She gasped. It was a deep gash, oozing with blood. He grimaced.

'That will need a stitch, but I don't have anything on me. I can wash it, wrap it up for now.'

'Good enough. Just make sure to tell the others you insisted,' he grunted.

And she smiled. 'Do you all have to act this tough all the time? It must be exhausting.' It made her wonder what feelings Fiske was trying to hide. Did he feel as though he had to put on a front with her?

She set to work on mopping up the blood and strapping up the wound. She was glad to have something to occupy her. Anything was better than having to sit next to Fiske, knowing that she still wanted him, but couldn't have him.

The other men passed her scraps of material and she was grateful to them for making her feel welcome. They weren't bad men at all, she thought.

'Do you have a wife—family—back at home?'

'Yes. And three children,' Arne said.

'How old?'

'They were just babes when I left. They'll be five, six and seven winters now.'

'You must have missed them desperately. Why did you leave?'

He looked at her, incredulous that she would ask such a thing. 'Because we are sworn to Fiske, Lady. We go where he goes.'

'You mean he forced you?' she asked, halting what she was doing. Surely he wouldn't be so cruel?

She looked up at Fiske at the prow, steering the boat, and he instantly turned away. He seemed angry, brooding. Well, so was she!

'No! We chose to. We would follow him anywhere. Lay down our lives for him. Our fates are all tied up to his destiny, as is yours now.'

She nodded. But was it? Would he want her to stay with him when they reached Denmark? The future felt so uncertain.

They rowed all day long, eventually coming to a large, beautiful lake. They moored the boat and the men began tearing off their clothes and jumping into the water in delight. Kassia saw her chance and went to climb out of the ship, but at the last moment, her arm was yanked back.

'Where do you think you're going?'

Fiske.

'To stretch my legs on dry land.'

'Had enough of touching my man?'

'What?' she asked.

'I'm surprised you don't want to stay and take a closer look at *him* without his clothes on.'

She shook her head, frowning at his childishness. 'I think you've had too much sun. I was just trying to help *your* injured man.'

He seemed angry as hell with her and she didn't know why. She was the one who was cross with him. The spike of irritation up her spine had her shrugging herself out of his arms, casting him off, and she stubbornly clambered out of the ship.

She began to walk at a pace, tearing off across the meadow in front of her, but he was right behind her.

'We need to stay by the boat. We don't know what tribes patrol this area.'

'You can.' She shrugged.

He tugged her arm again and she spun round, rounding on him. 'What do you want from me?' she snarled at him.

'Everything!'

And he hauled her to him, crushing her mouth with his. She tried to resist, pushing at his chest, turning her mouth away from him, still angry.

'You didn't this morning. You took what you wanted from me and then pushed me away.'

He reached for her again, pulling her up hard against his chest. 'I am nowhere near finished getting what I want—or need—from you, Kassia. I've barely even begun. I want you so much I can't even think straight. I could make love to you all day long and it probably still wouldn't satiate my desire for you.'

And as if to demonstrate it was the truth, he grabbed her bottom and pressed her belly into his groin, showing her just how much he desired her.

'I don't want there to be any space between us, no clothes, no breath, nothing.'

To prove it, he tugged her into a wooded grove and began to unbuckle her belt, his large hands trembling with need and urgency, as his mouth found her neck, her ears, her chest.

She realised protesting was futile, as she felt feverish, wanting him just as much. Unable to resist him, she fumbled with his own belt, pushing down his breeches as she felt her own slip over her legs, and he grabbed her bottom and lifted her, wrapping her legs around his waist, as he pressed her back against a tree. He made one hard thrust and plunged inside all the way, and her head tipped back on a rush of pleasure.

He felt so good. And with a groan of surrender he drove inside her again, the movement honest and raw and so intense it made her cry out in pleasure. He stormed her one more time and it tipped them over the edge. They both came apart, clinging to each other in euphoric desperation, and he whispered her name over and again into her hair.

He brought them down on to the ground, still holding her to him, their bodies quivering, their breathing erratic. And still buried inside her, he kissed her forehead, her cheeks and her nose. 'Are you all right?'

Her arms clasped around his neck and she nodded, attempting to get her breath back.

After a while, she placed her hand on his chest, looking up at him. 'Fiske...?'

He sighed. He knew it was time. She wanted to talk and he owed her an explanation. Especially after what they'd just done. He had to tell her the truth and deal with the consequences.

'Why did you pull away from me this morning, after everything that had happened between us?' she asked.

He stared down at her fingers on his chest, over his heart. He knew it was pounding. 'Because, for the first time in my life, I was afraid,' he said honestly. He placed his hands on her hips and lifted her off him, and she gasped at the loss of him. He set her down on the grass in front of him and she brought her knees up to her chest, curling her arms around them.

'Because I realised I've been unfair. I've allowed you to believe a lie about me, Kassia, when you've been nothing but truthful with me. I should have told you before last night...before I slept with you. Twice... Even before I married you, but I thought it might change how you felt about me.'

'What lie?'

'My father...he wasn't just a simple farmer who had his lands taken from him.'

She shook her head, as if she didn't understand what he was saying. A little crease appeared in her forehead and he wanted to kiss it away.

'My father was in line to be the next King of Denmark when he died.'

Her body stilled.

'When my grandfather died, before my father ascended the throne, my uncle attacked us, killing my father and stripping us of our wealth, lands and titles.'

She stared up at him, as if she couldn't believe what she was hearing.

'But we still have supporters. And I have my men. And it is my intention, when I get home, based on my new-found wealth and reputation, to raise an army and reclaim my throne. I intend to be King of Denmark some day soon, Kassia...and that would make you my Queen.'

Her ebony eyes were wide as she looked at him, shocked. Her mouth was working, but no sound was coming out.

'Why didn't you tell me this when we met?' she croaked eventually.

'It's not something I've ever had to worry about people minding about before… I didn't think it would be an issue. It wasn't until we were on the boat, leaving Constantinople, when you told me that you have never coveted a throne or wanted to wear a crown that I began to doubt what I'd done. That I should have told you from the start…but it never seemed to be the right time to broach it. Or perhaps I was just worried about your reaction if I did.'

'Did you think I would never find out?'

'I knew you would eventually. But we were getting on so well… I didn't want to ruin anything.'

There was a long silence as his words sank in… It felt good to have finally revealed his lineage, but he had no clue what she was going to say or do next. He couldn't bear to be parted from her, she consumed his every thought. He couldn't believe he'd even got jealous of her speaking to his friend, patching up his wound and making him smile. Was he going crazy?

His arm burned, his chest was in agony—but it would all pale into insignificance if she said she didn't want him now. If it wasn't the life she felt she could live, he would have to accept her decision, but he didn't know how he'd live without her. She was a part of him now, she was in his blood.

'I'm sorry, Kassia. I fear I have put you in danger. There will be a great battle before any of this comes to pass. I'm telling you now because I have friends in Lake Lagoda. I will understand if you don't want to come with me any further and I can leave you there in the knowledge you will be safe.'

He rubbed the back of his neck with his hand. 'Having done my part and got you far away from the Emperor and your family, we can divorce quietly—go our separate ways.'

She nodded, tears threatening to spill.

'But I want you to know, I want you at my side. I didn't say those marriage vows lightly. And I don't mean to break them. And whatever you might think, I believe you would make a wonderful Queen.'

Kassia's heart clamoured in her chest. Her body was still thrumming from their erotic outdoor lovemaking, feeling as though she never wanted to be parted from him, yet her thoughts were in chaos, running wild. She was reeling from what he had just told her.

Fiske was a prince of Denmark. A would-be king, making her his Queen. But she had been running from that very title since she'd met him... She had been trying to escape that future her whole life.

She had grown up knowing her parents wanted her to marry into royalty and she had fought it for all these years. It almost made her laugh bitterly to think of her mother's and father's faces if they were to find out she had married a future king.

She had never wanted to rule over people—she didn't want to stand out. She just wanted to live a normal life, to be free to behave as she wanted. She had been thinking that was how she could live with Fiske. Carefree. She had never wanted to live in a fortress or be excessively wealthy, and she didn't want the responsibility of having subjects, of ruling a country, of having to be someone to look up to.

And now she knew, if she continued on their journey to Denmark, when they reached his settlement, things would never be the same. They would be watched and scrutinised constantly. They would be in perpetual danger, as all monarchs are…

'I can't believe you lied to me,' she whispered.

He hung his head. 'I know, I'm sorry.'

Yet he had accepted her truth when she had told him about the Emperor. He had stuck by her. Could she do the same for him now? Wasn't that what a marriage was?

Now she knew why his lineage was so important. Why he might have wanted her to drink that tonic from the healer at the market the other day. Surely as a king, he could have no doubt about his children.

What he was telling her was huge. It sounded as if there was going to be a major battle in his fight for his crown and she had thought she had left all the bloodshed and brutality behind. But she knew she could not leave him to fight for his throne alone. No. She would stand by him as he had her, for as long as they were both able.

She reached out and put her hand to his cheek. 'I still want to come with you to Denmark. I still want to see where this journey takes us.' She wasn't ready to be parted from him.

He hauled her to him, wrapping her up in his strong embrace.

'Thank you.'

Besides, nothing was certain yet. She just knew she couldn't imagine her future without him in it.

Chapter Seven

The days on the boat turned into weeks as they followed the rivers and lakes north to the Baltic. The days were exhausting as they battled extreme weather and the fast-flowing currents, but each night when they moored upon a shore, Fiske and Kassia would slip away under cover of darkness to satiate themselves in each other's arms.

Fiske hated having to sneak around, having to take her wherever he could—in forests or in sandy bays. He longed to get her home and make love to her in a bed. He wanted to be able to touch her, be inside her, whenever he wanted.

Finally, on the thirtieth day, the shores of Aarhus came into view and he knew that, by the evening, they'd be dining at their settlement. There was much excitement on the boat among his men when they neared the rugged and familiar bay.

As they drew closer to the harbour, people began to spill out of their huts, to celebrate their return, waving and cheering. It was a glorious sight. There were more farmsteads than he remembered, more children playing on the beach. The people had been busy, he thought.

The men began launching themselves out of the ship, wading through the water to greet their wives and children, leaving Fiske to bring the vessel in to the jetty. But he didn't mind. It was the least he could do for the many winters' service they'd given him.

Then he saw his mother. Older, greyer, but her eyes still bright, her smile wide, surrounded by his sisters, and he grinned. It was so good to be home. He threw himself off the boat, tethering it to the jetty, and leaned down to help his bride out of the ship. He couldn't believe he had got her here, safe. And he couldn't wait to show her off.

His mother enveloped him in a giant hug and he squeezed her back, before introducing Kassia. 'Mother, sisters, meet my wife. This is Kassia, my Byzantine bride.'

'I knew someone would have to tame him some time,' his mother said, pulling her into a hug. 'Welcome.'

He enjoyed showing Kassia round the settlement, and she had been delighted to discover there was no palace, just a longhouse, where the people crammed inside to come together, eat and drink.

'It's nothing like Constantinople,' she'd told him, her face beaming. 'I like it a lot better.'

And he'd laughed, pleased she was happy.

The celebrations to mark the warriors' return lasted all day and he loved catching up with his family and his people. And he was glad they had all made Kassia feel at home, treating her kindly and with respect. He could tell they were in awe of her beauty, as was he, yet when they talked to her they discovered there was so much more to her, as had he.

Everyone was in good spirits, especially his men, content to be reunited with their women and children. But truth be told, Fiske was counting down the moments until he could be alone with his own wife. He had longed for this day since their wedding, to get her into his bed. Impatient, he made his way around the tables to where she stood, chatting in a group, and he came up behind her.

'Missing me?' he whispered in her ear.

She smiled and spun round. 'Actually, yes.'

'Want to get out of here?'

She nodded.

'It was a lavish homecoming,' she said, as he took her hand, leading her to a room at the back of the longhouse. 'A homecoming fit for a king.'

He grinned. 'It was, but all I really want to do is take my wife to bed.'

Shutting the door behind him, he leaned against it as she looked around. 'Alone at last.' He smiled.

'Is this your room?' she asked.

'*Our* room,' he said. 'Do you like it?'

She nodded. Her eyes ran over the furs on the bed and she licked her lips.

He closed the distance between them and kissed her, hard, on the mouth and suddenly she was kissing him back, her hands all over him, frantic with need, tugging his tunic out of his breeches and lifting it up, tugging it off, as if she was as desperate to see and touch his body again as he was hers. He laughed at her eagerness, but he understood it. He wanted to touch her freely, with no restraint. He wanted to take his time with her, not have a few rushed moments in a forest or on a beach.

His mouth was back on hers, grazing along her jaw and her neck as he grappled with the brooches holding up her pinafore. They sprang loose and he worked the material down, over her hips, sending it pooling to the floor. 'I miss you wearing my clothes,' he said. 'They were so much easier to dispose of!'

He gripped the hem of the tunic and pulled it up, over her arms and head, ruthlessly getting rid of it so she stood naked before him. Her breath hitched, but she didn't cover herself up. She stood there bravely before him, knowing he liked to look at her.

'I will never tire of seeing your body, Kassia,' he said.

He gripped her wrists and turned her round in his arms, so her back was pressed against him, his hard groin nestling against her beautiful buttocks. And he revelled in stroking his hands up her stomach and cupping her breasts, stimulating her nipples with his fingers, making her moan.

His hand roamed down to steal between her legs, his fingers stroking between her folds, and she whimpered, her knees buckling with the weight of her arousal. She was so wet…he knew she was ready for him. But tonight, he wanted to explore every part of his wife's body. He wanted to see her face as she came apart from all the delicious things he was going to do to her. He had been thinking of this night for weeks. It would be the first time he made love to her in a proper room, in a bed.

'Lie down, Kassia,' he whispered. 'On your front.'

She did as she was told, her naked body sprawled across the bed, her hair cascading across her shoulders. She looked back at him over her shoulder, her gaze heated, and he loved that she wasn't afraid of him, that she trusted him. It made him feel powerful. It made his desire soar.

He removed his own clothes and came towards her. His fingertips traced the line of her shoulders and down her back, before he lowered his head to follow the path with his lips. His masterful tongue glided all the way along her spine to the top of her buttocks and continued up over her cheeks.

'Fiske,' she whispered. 'Please. I want you.'

'Not yet.'

He turned her over and knelt before her, taking one of her ankles in his hand. He placed a kiss to the sensitive inside of her foot and she giggled, before he slid his tongue up her inner leg and her laughter turned to hectic, shallow breaths.

He allowed his eyes a moment to linger over her body, drinking it all in, trying to quench a thirst that could never seem to be quenched, before he loomed over her and ravished her breasts with his hot, swirling tongue. Her thrusting, tantalising nipples were pebble-hard and slick with his kisses, and she began to writhe beneath him, arching her back, wanting more.

Ruthlessly holding her squirming hips down, he

kissed his way down her body, over her taut stomach, and lower. When he reached his destination, he looked up at her from the apex of her thighs, their eyes meeting.

Finally, he placed his hot lips to her most secret, sensitive parts. Her alluring scent made him so painfully hard and he struggled to keep it together as his tongue curled around her sensitive nub, just as it had her nipples moments before. She cried out his name in shock and wonderment, bucking, before he flattened his tongue against her, tasting her fully.

When she tried to sit up, thrashing about, tugging at his shoulders and his head, he knew she was close. And when he felt her release against his lips, her legs trembling around his face, he still couldn't stop. He wouldn't. Not until he'd tasted every last drop of her...

Fiske looked up from his boat to see Kassia walking along the jetty towards him. They'd been home for a week and he was amazed that he still couldn't get enough of her. He wanted to be around her, talking to her, or touching her, all the time.

But today, he instantly knew something was wrong. Her face was pale, her lips taut. It was as if she was walking to her death.

'What is it?' he said, sitting up.

'Your mother has confirmed it.' Her voice sounded clipped, strange. 'She has told me I'm with child,' she said, twisting her hands in front of her, shuffling her feet.

The breath left him.

His tools clattered to the ground.

The sound of the ocean rushed in his ears.

He tried to recover himself and he curled out from the hull. He swung his leg around the prow and jumped out of the ship, coming to join her on dry land. So why did he feel as though he was sinking?

'You're with child?' His brows rose and he wiped his palm on his breeches.

She nodded, chewing her bottom lip.

'Is it his or mine?'

'I don't know,' she whispered miserably, shaking her head.

'Will we ever know?'

'I'm not sure.' A lone tear ran down her cheek and he couldn't bear to see her upset. Whatever he was feeling, he knew it was nothing compared to what she was going through. She must be in turmoil. He pulled her close, kissing her forehead.

'A baby is something to be celebrated, Kassia. And I hate to see you cry. This child will be loved no matter what. By both of us. All right?'

She nodded. 'Thank you,' she whispered, swiping away her tears.

'I feel like a fool for taking you on that journey now, in your condition.'

'You didn't know! And maybe I wasn't then?' she said hopefully. 'I really want it to be yours, Fiske. It would mean so much. And I know how important it is, given your lineage.'

He thought about how deeply he'd taken her during their first lovemaking and felt like a total brute. Had she been with child then? Or was he the one who had planted a seed inside her body that night? Or every night since. Surely the odds were in his favour?

He nodded. 'Me, too.'

And yet, even if it wasn't…he couldn't bring himself to regret the decisions he'd made. Given the choice again, he would make the same ones, if it meant being with her here, now.

Kassia couldn't sleep. It had been weeks and they'd barely touched since she'd told him she was with child. He had told her he didn't want to hurt her or the baby, but she wondered if that was his only reason. A great big chasm seemed to have opened up between them and she hated it. She wanted to stitch it back together with a giant needle.

She tossed and turned, worrying that her body was beginning to change—what if he didn't desire her any more? She had always hated being measured by her beauty but now, what if she lost the one thing that had made him take notice of her in the first place?

And what would happen when the baby came? What if it looked like Constantine? She wasn't sure she could love it. Surely Fiske wouldn't be able to either? And once word got out, his reputation would be ruined.

She was also excruciatingly aware that now her belly was swollen, growing by the day, his battle plans had been put on hold. He had said he couldn't leave her in her condition, but she knew he wasn't living the life for which he was intended. Being around her was holding him back and she could sense it in every word that was said between them, and every lack of touch. She saw his reluctance to leave, no doubt feeling responsible for her, but his men were waiting for him to lead them into battle, to finally claim what was his.

Deep down, she couldn't understand why Fiske would want to change all this...why this settlement wasn't enough for him, when everyone seemed perfectly happy. Or perhaps it was she who was happy, here, with him, and she didn't want him to go looking for more.

She felt she could live here for ever. She could ride and swim and she didn't think she would ever get tired of the views over the ocean. She found it no hardship to help with the land and the animals. For the first time, she had so many friends. And she had him...only he wasn't content.

She knew she had to put his happiness before her own, as he had done for her these past weeks. Because if you loved someone, that's what you did, wasn't it? And she loved him with every breath she took. She had loved him from the first moment she'd seen him on that boat. So she lay there plucking up the courage, trying to stop her heart from breaking, for she knew she had to do something awful. She knew she had to make him despise her, so that he'd leave her.

With pain tearing her apart, finally, she woke him.

'What is it? Are you and the baby all right?' he asked, sitting up in bed.

She nodded. She didn't know how to do this. All she knew was that she must, otherwise he'd end up resenting her—and the baby.

'Arne told me your men are ready—waiting for word that you'll take them into Aarhus and fight your uncle. Why haven't you left yet?'

He frowned. 'I can't leave you in your condition.'

'Can't, or won't? I know you think you need to be here for me, but I'm fine. Really. I don't need you, but your men—your people—do.'

'Are you trying to get rid of me?' He tried to smile and failed.

'Fiske, your army is waiting. It is time to go and take back what was stolen from you.'

He shook his head. 'I'm not leaving you,' he said instinctively. And she could have wept. Did he love her, too?

'Are you really willing to give up your chance to be King to stay by my side while I have this baby?' It pained her to say the next part. 'A baby we don't even know is yours?'

He reeled. 'Don't say that.'

But she forced herself to continue. 'Why not? It's the truth. This baby probably isn't yours, is it? And it could ruin your lineage. Do you really want the Emperor's child sitting on your throne?'

His face darkened.

'Besides, you know I've never wanted to be Queen. It was only a matter of time… You said I would be free to make my own choice when we arrived here, and I've decided I don't want this any more. *Us.*'

He paled, shaking his head. 'Why are you saying all this now?'

Seeing the hurt in his eyes, she felt that this was the worst thing she'd ever done.

'Because I can't live like this, pretending that we're something we're not… Things will only get worse between us when the baby is born.'

'Are you saying you don't want me?' He got out of bed and began throwing on his clothes, angrily. 'If you are, I need to hear you say it.'

She stood, too, on the other side of the bed. Her legs were shaking so much she was worried they might give way. She tried to swallow down her torment, her throat thick with tears. Was this the last time she'd ever see his beautiful body unclothed? 'I don't think either of us knows what we want right now. And I think it would be better if you left.'

He belted up his breeches with an air of finality. 'You want me to leave?'

'Yes.'

His throat worked. 'If I go, I won't be coming back…'

'I know that,' she said, her voice raw. 'But you don't belong here… I think you should go.'

'I need to hear you say it, Kassia.'

'I don't want you,' she whispered. 'I don't want the life you want for us.'

And he blanched. 'Very well then,' he said coldly.

He stalked over to the door, pulling it open. And then he stilled. He turned and lifted a hand to curve over her face. 'The silver your father gave me for your dowry is in my boat. If something happens to me, you'll need it.'

She felt as if her emotions were strangling her. 'But

I thought you used it to raise an army... I thought that's why you married me?' she whispered.

'No, Kassia. It was never about that,' he said, running his knuckles down her cheek, before leaning in and pressing a kiss against her forehead. Her breath caught. And when he closed the door behind him, she broke down, slumping to the floor and sobbing until she felt hollow inside.

Chapter Eight

They'd been fighting for months and Fiske was bone-achingly weary. But the end was in sight; he could feel it in his bones. Looking all around him, they were almost through the fortress walls. He and his men could finish this, today.

Kassia's words had tormented him throughout the winter and with every blow of his sword, he had tried to block out his hurt. Spring was now on the horizon, but his heart still hadn't thawed. Her words had wounded him, more than any injury he'd ever suffered in battle.

But what he couldn't be sure of was had she deceived him about her feelings so he would leave, concerned for him and his own destiny? He hoped he hadn't put everything at risk for his desire to claim back his crown... Or had she meant what she'd said? That she didn't want him. He didn't want to believe it, yet she had been adamant.

Buildings were burning and men were fighting in one-to-one vicious combat. The fortress had been under siege all winter and he knew their supplies were running low. Sickness within the walls was rife. It was only a matter of time… He hoped his uncle would see sense and yield soon—he certainly didn't want any more villagers to die on his account. And he wanted there to be a fortress left for him to rule over.

They had been using a battering ram for days, making steady progress, but all of a sudden the gates gave way, splintering into pieces. After a moment of disbelief, his soldiers collected themselves and charged, racing into the fortress square and continuing their affront inside.

Fiske held his sword high in one hand and threw himself into the fray. He couldn't give up now, not when he was so close. Right beside him, his men were fighting just as furiously, as always. They had been nothing less than stoic. And he so desperately wanted to reward them with lands and titles when he came to power. The thirty of them at the front were a sight to behold and it soon became clear the enemy's army was overrun. No one seemed to have the stomach to fight them, not when they'd seen Fiske leading so determinedly. And slowly, incredibly, all around them, his uncle's men began to lay down their weapons, finally bending the knee and asking for forgiveness.

Arne and Erik disappeared into the hall, reappearing moments later bundling his uncle forwards, forcing him down on to the ground. Had the man been cowering inside, letting his men fight for him? What a coward!

Anger licked through Fiske's veins. His uncle had been the cause of all his family's grief and pain. He had stolen his father and his birthright from him and he could never forgive him for it. He did not deserve to rule Aarhus. But holding the tip of his blade against his enemy's neck, he had a decision to make.

'Go on, Fiske. Do it,' his uncle goaded him.

But Fiske had seen enough bloodshed these past six winters. And he didn't want to start his reign in the same way his uncle had. He wanted his rule to be one of peace and mercy.

'No. I will not kill you. You will be allowed to live, with your shame, to watch how this country should be run. To see it prosper and its people happy. They will know from the off that I am a better man than you and will be a far better king.'

Fiske and his men dined heartily that night and rejoiced in their achievements. He had finally done it and it felt good to be back in his grandfather's great hall. To have avenged his father's death. Now all he needed was for his mother and his sisters to join them. For all the men's families to arrive, to make this place a home again. But mainly, he wanted his wife at his side… Would she agree to rule with him here?

He couldn't wait any longer to find out. He couldn't bear to be parted from her any longer.

'Erik, ride out to the settlement immediately. Tell them all to pack their things, that we shall be coming for them on the morrow.'

The men looked between each other.

'Your Highness…' Arne said, clearing his throat, leaning forward across the table. 'We didn't want to tell you until after the battle. We thought it would affect your focus.'

He studied them. 'Tell me what?'

'It's Kassia…'

His veins iced over. 'What is it?'

'Your wife gave birth a few weeks ago, Your Highness… A healthy boy.'

His heart slammed in his chest. A son?

'But Kassia…'

His whole body tensed. 'What about her?'

'It was a difficult birth. She's not well…'

Fiske launched out of his seat in panic and fury. 'How sick? Why are you only telling me this now?'

Fear was lashing through him. Was she going to survive? He needed all the details. Now.

'We knew you would put her before the cause, Your Highness. We didn't want you to give up after you had come so far… She wouldn't have wanted that.'

'And how do *you* know what my wife wants?' he raged, furious with his men, for thinking they knew best. How *dare* they?

'She made me promise, before we left, that I would help you see it through,' Arne said. 'That I wouldn't let you go back, no matter what.'

He swallowed, appalled, yet a glimmer of hope tried to break through his fear, like sunlight breaking through a gap in the clouds. Perhaps the things she had said when she'd told him to leave had been for his benefit. Perhaps she hadn't really meant them.

'And where do your loyalties lie?'

'With both of you. My King and Queen. We all have

the greatest respect for Her Highness, mainly because she knows you better than anyone, and she has your best interests at heart.'

He felt the ice in his heart begin to crack. And it hurt. He didn't care about anything that had passed before. He just wanted to get back to her, to make sure she was all right.

'Rally the men. Ready the horses.'

Arne smiled. 'I take it the celebrations are over? That we're heading back to the settlement?'

'We leave immediately.'

Kassia tugged the blanket tighter around herself as she watched the sun set over the ocean. She loved this place. Denmark was her home now, where she belonged. It was where her friends and family were. It was where the man she loved had lived with her for a while.

Thoughts of Fiske filled her mind. Her love for him hadn't lessened over the months they'd been apart; it had only grown, and she longed to see him again. To tell him she was sorry about everything she had said before and to tell him how she really felt.

She cradled her sleeping son closer, wanting to keep him warm. Finally, the last signs of winter were receding. It had been a difficult few months, every landmark covered in snow, as if preserving her memories, tormenting her with what she had lost.

Now, as the last of the day's warmth ebbed away, she shuddered and rose to her feet, heading back to the settlement. Shrouded in near darkness, the longhouse loomed before her. She paused for a moment, taking a breath before she entered. She wasn't ready to say good-bye to the people. It was going to be hard.

Drawing on his strength, it was Fiske's face she thought about as she pushed open the doors and stepped inside. It was his face she thought about as she walked through the bustling crowd. And when she raised her head, she gasped. It was his face she saw.

Fiske.

Fiske was striding down the hall towards her.

He was here.

Her footsteps faltered, just like the first time, when she saw him at the bride show. Her legs almost gave way—she was so weak still from the birth—but he was at her side in an instant, bolstering her with his brilliant blue gaze.

He took her by the elbow, holding her up, and she wanted to throw her arms around him, but she knew she could not, not in front of all these people. She didn't know whether he wanted her to.

'I heard you weren't well. I came as quickly as I could…' Then he pulled her and the baby to him, enveloping them in his arms, surprising her, kissing her forehead.

She gave a sob of release. She couldn't believe he was here, holding her. It was as if she'd conjured him up by thinking about him.

He pulled away from her to look into her eyes. 'Are you all right?'

She shook her head. 'They are tears of relief and happiness. I'm just so delighted to see you,' she cried.

'What are *you* doing here? Is it really true? Did you avenge your father?'

He nodded. 'Yes. It took a while, but the throne of Denmark is now mine…'

'All hail the King of Denmark!' Arne shouted and the people repeated the words, kneeling, all around them.

Fiske nodded his thanks, touched, but his attention quickly came back to Kassia. 'Do you need to sit?'

She shook her head. 'I'm better now. We had heard that you were close to taking the fortress and I was preparing to leave here and come and find you… I had to see you. I couldn't bear it any longer. But now you're here… I don't understand,' she said, shaking her head. 'What *are* you doing here?'

'Surely you know…?' He inclined his head. 'You're more important to me than any crown or country, Kassia. I may have my own kingdom and people to rule, but that's nothing without my family at my side. I came here for you.'

She released a long breath she felt she'd been holding all winter, almost wilting in relief.

'Fiske… I didn't mean any of those things I said that night. I just didn't want to keep you here and hold you back. I had to set you free…'

'I know,' he said, kissing her forehead again, pulling her closer. 'I've had a long time to think about it all. But I want you to know I'd give up my crown to spend my life with you. You come before all else. And from now on, I want us to walk the same path. I don't ever want to be parted from you again.'

He dropped down on to one knee, along with the rest of his subjects. 'I should have done this from the moment I met you. Told you of my desires and waited for your answer. Will you be my wife and my Queen, Kassia, now that Denmark is ours?'

She stared down at him, tears filling her eyes.

'I know it's not the life you thought you wanted…'

'It is more than I could ever have dreamed of.' She laughed. 'Yes, Fiske. Of course I will.'

He rose and kissed her fully on the mouth then, opening her lips and tangling his tongue with hers, not caring that everyone was watching, as if he wanted them all to know how much he loved her. But the child between them began to gurgle and he pulled away, his eyes dropping to the bundle in her arms.

'So this is your son?' He smiled. 'Does he have a name?'

'*Your* son. His name's Baldur,' she answered and she saw him draw breath. She had chosen a traditional Danish name that meant Prince. 'Your mother helped me choose it.'

She pulled the blankets away from around the baby's face so Fiske could see him. And she saw his eyes widen, knew he was taking it in. The child had the same deep dimple as him, in the middle of his chin, and matching brilliant blue eyes.

'Do you want to hold him?'

Fiske nodded, tears brimming. And they knew, instinctively, when he held the boy in his arms, that he was his.

'He looks just like you,' Kassia said, laughing. 'I love him so much, because I love his father so deeply.'

He drew her towards him for another kiss, holding his wife and his son in his arms. 'I love you, too, Kassia. I loved you since the moment I saw you, when you tried to steal my ship. I loved you at the bride show the instant I saw you walk across the stage. I loved you when you agreed to come away with me, stamped your foot at me and watched me take a shower.' He grinned. 'And I loved you as your belly blossomed, despite not knowing whose child you were carrying.' He pulled away slightly to look into her eyes. 'I chose you to be my wife, and my Queen, Kassia, and it's the best decision I've ever made. Thank you so much for agreeing to be mine.'

* * * * *

If you enjoyed these stories, make sure to pick up Lucy Morris's Shieldmaiden Sisters trilogy

The Viking She Would Have Married
Tempted by Her Outcast Viking
Beguiling Her Enemy Warrior

And check out one of Sarah Rodi's great reads

One Night with Her Viking Warrior
Claimed by the Viking Chief
Second Chance with His Viking Wife

COMING NEXT MONTH FROM

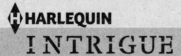

HARLEQUIN

INTRIGUE

#2199 A PLACE TO HIDE
Lookout Mountain Mysteries • by Debra Webb
Two and a half years ago, Grace Myers, infant son in tow, escaped a serial killer. Now, she'll have to trust Deputy Robert Vaughn to safeguard their identities and lives. The culprit is still on the loose and determined to get even...

#2200 WETLANDS INVESTIGATION
The Swamp Slayings • by Carla Cassidy
Investigator Nick Cain is in the small town of Black Bayou for one reason—to catch a serial killer. But between his unwanted attraction to his partner Officer Sarah Beauregard and all the deadly town secrets he uncovers, will his plan to catch the killer implode?

#2201 K-9 DETECTION
New Mexico Guard Dogs • by Nichole Severn
Jocelyn Carville knows a dangerous cartel is responsible for the Alpine Valley PD station bombing. But convincing Captain Baker Halsey is harder than uncovering the cartel's motive. Until the syndicate's next attack makes their risky partnership inevitable...

#2202 SWIFTWATER ENEMIES
Big Sky Search and Rescue • by Danica Winters
When Aspen Stevens and Detective Leo West meet at a crime scene, they instantly dislike each other. But uncovering the truth about their victim means combining search and rescue expertise and acknowledging the fine line between love and hate even as they risk their lives...

#2203 THE PERFECT WITNESS
Secure One • by Katie Mettner
Security expert Cal Newfellow knows safety is an illusion. But when he's tasked with protecting Marlise, a prosecutor's star witness against an infamous trafficker and murderer, he'll do everything in his power to keep the danger—and his heart—away from her.

#2204 MURDER IN THE BLUE RIDGE MOUNTAINS
The Lynleys of Law Enforcement • by R. Barri Flowers
After a body is discovered in the mountains, special agent Garrett Sneed returns home to work the case with his ex, law enforcement ranger Madison Lynley. Before long, their attraction is heating up...until another homicide reveals a possible link to his mother's unsolved murder. And then the killer sets his sights on Madison...

HICNM0124

Get 3 FREE REWARDS!

We'll send you 2 FREE Books plus a FREE Mystery Gift.

FREE Value Over **$20**

Both the **Harlequin® Historical** and **Harlequin® Romance** series feature compelling novels filled with emotion and simmering romance.